The Adventure
By
Ashley Nemer

ART OF SAFKHET

MAVERICK TOUCH THE ADVENTURE
Version 2
Edited by Katia Vodin
Cover Stacy A. Moran
Copyright © 2015 Ashley Nemer
www.ashleynemer.com[1]
All rights reserved.

No part of this book may be reproduced except small excerpts for review purposes without the expressed written consent of the author. This includes any reproductions by forms including but not limited to electronic and mechanical.

A product of the Art of Safkhet
www.artofsafkhet.com[2]
ISBN-13: 978-1941194058
ISBN-10: 1941194052
BISAC: Fiction / Mystery & Detective / Women Sleuths
Published May, 2015

---

1. http://www.ashleynemer.com
2. http://www.artofsafkhet.com

DEDICATION

I want to thank my Grandma Elsie. While this book should have been a simple project, it took four times as long as it ought to have, and my grandma helped to keep me encouraged each step of the way.

Thank you for always encouraging and supporting me, Grandma.

This one's for you.

"Heaven knows we need never be ashamed of our tears, for they are rain upon the blinding dust of earth, overlying our hard hearts." – Charles Dickens, Great Expectation.

CHAPTER ONE

"Life has a way of changing right before people's eyes, and you never know when it will happen." Nadia read over the start of her news article a few times. The first line didn't seem grabbing enough, but she was determined to get it finished today. She had promised Scully a travel story featuring the places in Africa that they were visiting, and in exchange, a nice new desk and expense account were awaiting her return.

He was trying to keep her happy. Nadia had been considering a career change, something to keep her a bit safer, and Scully was fighting it every step of the way. She had first tried to leave when she had won the lottery a few years ago, but the drama had sucked her back in, and of course the fact she hadn't won enough money to keep her clothed and fed for more than a couple years. It wasn't like she had won the mega millions lotto. Gabe, her best friend, kept telling her she loved the thrill of the action too much to leave, and that would always keep her in the limelight.

Now, Carlisle wanted her safe. Her parents wanted her safe. She wanted her safe. Everything still felt fresh from her trip to Houston and even her abduction a year or two before. Her need for action and adventure had begun to subside.

Then, of course, there was the other issue, the one she hadn't told Carlisle about yet. She hadn't told anyone, except her doctor, although technically her doctor had told her at her annual check-up.

Nadia brought her mind back to focus on the news article. She used to love the travel pieces for the simple fact she got to experience so many different things in life. She really had an internal struggle in the decision to step back from the news. Africa was a beautiful place. There were jungles on one side and plains on another. They had been expecting lots of wilderness and having to 'rough it,' but they hadn't expected so much luxury in the hotel accommodations.

Carlisle never short changed anything. He always went all out, but she could still be surprised by his actions, and these accommodations topped her expectations.

There was a knock on the door before she saw Anabella stick her head inside. "Hey, sis, you ready? I hear there is a hungry hungry hippo waiting our arrival."

Nadia laughed and turned away from her laptop to look at her sister. "Really, Ana? You sound like a television commercial." Her hand absently went down to her stomach, and she placed a protective hand on top of it. She hadn't yet told anyone what was going on, but since this would be her last adventure, she was going to enjoy these moments with her sister.

Anabella pushed open the door and came walking into the room, smiling. "It made you laugh, so I did my job. You look too stressed to be on vacation."

"You did. Give me a sec. I'm working on this article so I can send it off. I'm just about done." Pregnancy hormones had kicked in two weeks ago, and since then, she had become easily distracted. "Give me a sec," was a something of a generous estimate. It would actually be a miracle if she managed to finish her article.

"News articles are your kryptonite, you know that?"

"Why do you say that?" She looked up at her sister and subconsciously she felt like she had a look of guilt on her face. She hated hiding big news, but it just wasn't the right time. Anabella typically knew when Nadia had something up her sleeve, but thankfully, since Carter came into the picture, Anabella's observation skills had been lacking.

Her sister shook her head back and forth. "The room could be on fire, and you would still be working on your laptop. Come on, close it down, and let's go see the hippo."

"The stories are important to me. I can't help it. It's like you and the martial arts. A guy could be holding a gun, and you'd bring your fists out."

Both sisters laughed as Nadia closed her laptop and put her shoes on. "Did you grab your camera?"

Anabella reached into her shoulder bag, pulled out her single lens reflector digital camera, and raised it up to show Nadia. "Yep."

"Dang, could your lens be any larger?" It looked like it stuck out five inches from the base of the camera.

"It's an 800 zoom lens. I don't know about you, but I don't want to get too close to any hippo."

"Good point. Glad you're on top of things."

They made their way out of the room and down the hall where they met Carlisle and Carter in the concierge lounge. They were both dressed in comfortable yet expensive attire. Carlisle had on khaki pants with a blue and white button-down shirt, and Carter had on a green cardigan with a white polo and Calvin Klein jeans.

"Ladies," Carter said as he raised his glass up in the air, saluting their entrance.

"Are you two ready to start the adventure of a lifetime?" Carlisle calmly said as he wrapped his arm around Nadia's waist and pulled her close to kiss the top of her head.

"I thought that's what this trip was to begin with, an adventure," Nadia said in a cool reply.

"It is, my pet, but now we will be trekking our way into the wilderness where danger may loom in every corner. You must be very careful."

Carlisle's voice had a way of taking a calm tone and adding some sort of sinister vibe to it.

"Sounds like you two just want to scare us," Anabella told Carter as she ran her hand down the front of his shirt.

"A bit of healthy fear is good for anyone. Now come on. We got the jeep ready to rock and roll," Carter replied, giving a sinister smile.

The four of them turned towards the door and started walking out of the lounge, headed towards the elevator. As they walked up, the elevator doors slid open, and after the patrons inside stepped out, the four of them went inside and began their first adventure in Africa.

Hot summer days in Africa were completely different from the hot summer days in Houston. Carter's body would eventually adjust to the different temperatures, but until then, he would be constantly wiping the sweat off of his brow. He wasn't sure whose idea it had been to go out on a safari in search of the hippos. From what he had read, this particular animal was the most dangerous one they could possibly encounter.

"Carter, the girls want to get close enough for a picture with the hippo."

Hearing Carlisle's voice brought Carter back to the actions at hand, the jeep ride through the jungle. "Absolutely not."

"See, you two are crazy. We won't let you risk your lives just for a photo."

"No way, Ana, this sounds like a trumped up idea Nadia would come up with. You're smarter than that!" Carter declared.

"Hey!" Nadia protested. "I take offense to that."

"It was your idea," Anabella whispered.

"See!" Carter said, tossing his hands in the air. "No way, no how. Not happening!"

"Ana, I'm confused. Who died and made them the boss of us?" Nadia had an indignant tone.

"I became your boss the day you decided to join that chatroom." Carlisle's eyes squinted as he looked down on Nadia. His lips curved up in a sinister grin, and Carter couldn't help letting out a laugh.

"Calm down, Mr. A. I'm sure the girls didn't mean to drive us to drink so early in on our trip, right ladies?" Carter kept his tone neutral. He didn't want to encourage their crazy ideas, but he didn't want to come down on them hard either.

"Always the level minded man, Mr. J," Carlisle retorted. "Nadia, you may see the hippos from a safe distance through your sister's lens, agreed?"

Nadia nodded her head. It was plain to see by the look on her face that she was reluctant to give into her husband's wishes. "Agreed."

"Now that this is settled, are you two enjoying married life?" Anabella chuckled as she snuggled herself into Carter's arms.

He loved when she leaned on him for anything. It had been tough to get her to drop her walls, but now that he had her, he wasn't going to let her go. She always smelled of soap. Not the medical smell of soap, but the sweet lavender scent. It reminded Carter of his mother.

In reality, a lot of what Anabella was reminded him of his mother, if he was honest with himself, from her natural scent to her compassionate, loving nature. He hadn't spent a lot of time in the past thinking about the woman who had been taken from him at such a young age. Every time he watched or read anything about Batman, he couldn't help feeling sorry for Bruce Wayne. He knew what it was like to be that orphan.

While Bruce's family had been taken at one time, his family hadn't been so lucky. His mother had been driving home from dropping him off at a friend's house when she'd gotten a flat tire. She'd been kneeling on the ground, changing the tire, when a teenage boy had lost control of his car and hit her. She'd been sandwiched between the two vehicles.

His eyes always watered when he thought about her beautiful body smashed between those two metal, tank-like vehicles. Like Bruce, who felt the guilt for needing to leave the theater where his parents were then mugged and killed, Carter felt guilty that had he had needed to go out to his friend's house that night. If he hadn't, she wouldn't have picked up the nail in the tire that had caused the flat.

He'd gone to therapy, where they had continued to tell him it wasn't his fault. It's never the child's fault. The only one who agreed with him was his father, who then became the town drunk. Where most men didn't leave their house without a wallet, Carter's father never left home without a flask.

Each weekday there would be a different liquid in the container. The range went from vodka to whisky and anything in between. The nights that it was Patron were the nights that Carter dreaded most of all, Wednesdays. On those days, Carter always made a point to stay late at school or find some extracurricular sport he could participate in as long as possible.

This plan worked until Carter turned sixteen and wanted more freedom. He wanted his license, but his father wasn't having that. He made him suffer as much as he could, forcing him to have the neighbors take him out for his driving tests.

On his eighteenth birthday, he finally had saved enough money to purchase a used vehicle. He found a random used car, a beat up Dodge truck. He handed the salesman a thousand dollars, filled out some paperwork, and took off east.

He was from a small town in the hill country of Texas. He drove down Interstate-45 for a few hours until he landed in Houston, where he found a job and a place to stay. It was when he met Ivy that his life really changed. She was the one who had led him to Carlisle and the brotherhood. Even now, decades later, thinking back on his start, he felt his eyes get misty.

Ivy had been in her mid-forties when they'd first met, but she hadn't looked a day over twenty-seven. Her skin had been as smooth as a baby's, her hair fire red. She'd enjoyed being that shockingly beautiful woman in the room. Ivy had taken him under her wing and taught him how to survive. Her brother was Abraham. Carter never had gotten a first name from him, but Abraham was in charge of the North American brotherhood. They were the two who trained everyone and ensured they got paid.

Thinking about his start, where he had come from, made Carters chest pull tight. He heard himself suck in a deep breath and let it out calmly.

"You okay, honey?" Anabella whispered in his ear.

Carter realized that his eyes gave him away to her every time. He had told her about his past when she'd asked how he and Carlisle had become acquaintances. She knew him well enough now that hiding things like this from her was out of the question. With a slow nod, he nuzzled his head against hers and softly replied back, "Yeah, just thinking about Mom."

She cupped a hand over his cheek and said, "She would be proud of you, you know that, right?"

"Yeah. Doesn't make it any easier that every time I take in the scent of you. It reminds me of how much I loved her."

She placed a soft kiss on his lips and nuzzled him back. "I understand. I wish I could have met her."

"Me too. You would have loved her."

"I'm sure I would have."

Carter let the remainder of the drive go by without further thought of his troubled past. He wasn't the same boy he'd been when he left Bandera, Texas. He was a man now, and men didn't let silly things like the past haunt them forever.

"Nadia, you writing anything about the adventure for the paper?"

She turned around from the front seat and smiled at Carter. "Yeah, I am. In fact, Ana interrupted me as I was trying to come up with a way to complete my news article. You know I love my travel section. Scully always gives me plenty of freedom; I just don't know what angle I want to take, like with the Houston one, I did the homeless. What cause do I want to push this time? You know?"

Carlisle was quick to respond. "You know, you don't have to have any specific angle. You could simply write a news report on how beautiful this country is. I mean, look at all of the nature passing us by as we drive to these hippos."

Carter watched Nadia shrug her shoulders.

"Something tells me Nadia is the kind of girl who likes causing trouble with her writing, otherwise she doesn't have any fun," he said.

Everyone in the jeep laughed, and then, off to the right, they saw the lake that they were told about back at the hotel. It was too far off in the distance to see a clear view of the animals, but they were close.

"Ana, get out your camera!" Nadia said.

"On it!" Anabella replied.

Carlisle slowed the jeep down and cautiously turned off the road and onto the off-road path, heading towards the lake. The horizon looked serene. There was wildlife roaming the grounds in each direction they looked. The birds overhead were swooping and soaring, their colors making a vivid contrast to the clear blue sky.

"They are so beautiful," Nadia said as she stepped outside of the jeep after Carlisle parked the vehicle.

"Hard to believe we live on the same planet when you see nature like this," Anabella replied as she walked over to her sister.

"Humans will be the destruction of this land," Carter said in a slightly lowered volume.

"Don't be such a pessimistic man," Anabella told him.

He shrugged. "Nature of the job."

"That's why what we do is so important. Have to get rid of the trash of society one way or another so we can preserve it for your nephews and future generations." Carlisle had walked over to the sisters and wrapped his arm around Nadia. "Right, my pet?"

"I suppose. I just… I want to enjoy the beauty of this land."

"Enjoy away. Don't let a couple of grumpy old men stop you."

"Speak for yourself, Carlisle! I may be grumpy, but I am far from an old man."

"Depends on who you're asking," Anabella teased him as she gave him a soft elbow to the side.

"Well, I see where I stand with this crowd. Guess I'll just stay in the jeep while you three go enjoy yourselves. Carlisle, don't forget to take your walking cane for balance. Hate to see you throw out a hip."

Everyone laughed at one another, and then as a group, they began to gradually walk towards the lake.

"Stop right there, that's perfect," Anabella said to Nadia. She had her hands held up in a square shape with her thumbs and forefingers touching. "That will make a great picture. It could go on the front page of the travel section for your news article." She brought her camera up to her face and zoomed in with her lens. With a few adjustments, she caught Nadia in her leather jacket with her arms crossed, smiling at the camera just as one of the hippos was opening his mouth in the lake. It was a perfectly placed work of angles.

"Got it?" Nadia asked.

"Yep, and I'm sure this is going to look fantastic. I worked it so you looked like you were standing right in front of the hippo."

"Awesome, can't wait to see it." Nadia walked over to her sister and looked down at the digital viewing screen of her single lens reflector camera. "How could you see anything, the sun is so bright it's flushing the screen out."

"I had to look through the peep hole. Trust me, it's perfect. I'll show you when I get back to the hotel."

"I will have to come up with some great story about us being on a safari to go with that image. Damn, I should have brought a camo jacket and not my leather one."

"I'm surprised you haven't melted away in it yet," Carter chimed in.

"How many times do I have to tell everyone, I go everywhere with this baby. It's gotten me through many rough times."

"Sis, it's time to retire the jacket," Anabella teased.

Nadia wiggled her finger at her sister and grinned. "Don't get me started on the bad habits that you need to give up, missy. I'll call Kain right now, and we will start listing them all."

"Them all?! Are you crazy? I don't have any bad habits."

Carter chuckled under his breath, and everyone turned and looked at him. Anabella raised her eyebrow and tilted her head to the side. "Excuse me, is there something we need to discuss in private?"

"No, no. Nothing at all, I promise, babe!" He held his hands up in the air as if saying he surrendered.

"Don't you 'babe' me. Speak now or forever hold your peace, Carter Jackson!"

Anabella saw out of the corner of her eye that Nadia had moved closer to Carlisle, and they had started walking off on their own towards the forest. She turned her attention back to Carter and began to walk forward.

"I promise, Ana, I love everything about you. I was just laughing. There isn't anything I would change. Except for that evil eye. It would scare even the Dali Lama."

That made her laugh. She reached him and then wrapped her arms around his midsection. "I'll accept that answer, but you have to remember you are always on my side when it comes to Nadia. Never show weakness!"

"She is family, Ana. It's not a competition."

Shaking her head, Anabella said, "You don't know women at all."

"Well, let us be fair, does any man really know women?"

"Good point. Let's go join them."

The four of them stopped three hundred yards away from the hippos. They stood there in silence, enjoying nature. Soon there were giraffes that had made their way to the water and were now enjoying the refreshment the lake provided.

"We should have brought a picnic," Nadia said.

"Ten steps ahead of you," Carter replied as he turned around and jogged back to the jeep. The three of them waited patiently as Carter rummaged around the trunk of the jeep and then made his way back to them with a large cooler in hand. "Dinner is served."

He placed the cooler on the ground and opened it. He pulled out a blanket that he handed to Carlisle to spread out. Pretty soon the men had four place settings all laid out with food, utensils, and beverages.

There wasn't anything quite like a picnic in Africa with your family. Anabella looked around at Carter and then the animals. She hadn't realized how much he had begun to mean to her until this moment. Somewhere along the line, things had changed. She just wasn't quite sure when that was.

CHAPTER TWO

Picnics and hippos were a great way for the group to not only work up an appetite for dinner but also to enjoy time together as couples. The four of them were able to break off into pairs and spend time with one another without any interruptions. On the way back to the hotel, they enjoyed talking about the sisters' parents. William and Laura always traveled the world. While growing up, Nadia and Anabella envied their mother's ability to be so carefree and travel to anyplace that she desired.

They had always wanted to marry men who would be able to provide them that same type of experiences that their mother had found. Anabella wasn't jealous of Nadia, exactly, for finding Carlisle. At first, the whole situation with Mr. A had put all of them on guard. None of them were exactly sure that he would be good for her, but after two years, she had come to be an active member of their relationship, and while sometimes Anabella felt like the third wheel, that feeling had lessened since Carter had become such a prevalent person in their lives.

Anabella had first thought he was a bit extravagant. His house in Houston was a mansion, and not a small sized one, but a very large plot of land. Often times, it felt to her like she was staying in a resort when she was there visiting. He had wanted her to quit her job so she could travel around the world with him and live with him in Houston. It was tempting. She loved the appeal of traveling but had to keep her feet grounded. That was part of why they had come with Carlisle and Nadia to Africa, or rather, they had come with her. Either way, the four of them were here now, and they were enjoying it.

She had enjoyed this afternoon. It was a good balance of time with Nadia and then time with Carter. The men seemed to time everything just right so the transitions from one thing to another went very smoothly. At times it unnerved both women how alike the two men were. Anabella knew that came from training. When you trained long enough with someone, you began to pick up shared habits.

The knowledge that the two of them were at least close enough to be so much alike gave her comfort, knowing that even though these men were killers, they were still able to maintain relationships and bond with other people. To some strangers, this whole situation would be highly unusual, but the reality was that circumstances like this were quite normal in everyday modern societies.

Laura and Anabella had gotten into a large debate over it two Christmas ago. It had ended up being a huge family debacle that now no one mentioned. For a while, Anabella had worried she had alienated Carlisle and her mother, but after months of no one bringing it back up, it seemed things had smoothed over.

Carlisle's first Christmas participation with the family, after Nadia had gotten kidnapped and he'd saved her, had been quite unusual. No one would admit that Nadia and Mr. A had feelings for one another and that they were dating. It was a widely known fact among their family, but the two of them hadn't publically acknowledged it. During the family dinner, Anabella had asked Carlisle if he and Nadia were seriously dating or still in denial.

That led to Laura chiming in that one simply didn't date an assassin. Anabella then brought up that for millennia women had dated mafia members and leaders of secret societies. How would dating an assassin be any different? Laura insisted this was different because people were typically born into those families. Anabella remembered how the conversation went. It was as if it had happened yesterday.

"Anabella, there have not been millennia of people dating assassins. Stop filling your sister's head with that," Laura spouted out during the heated argument.

"Mom, you're wrong! Look at Italy. How old is the mafia? What about Russia? The Czars, dictators, or the family heads? Someone had to date and marry them at one point! It's in our nature to seek out bad boys."

Everyone turned to look at Carlisle, who simply shrugged and said, "I don't expect people to understand or like me. I just expect you to stay out of my way."

The tension at the dinner table could be cut with a knife. The thickness loomed in the air.

"Mom, behave..." Nadia said firmly.

"I'm not saying I have anything against Carlisle. We all enjoy having him in your life. What I am saying is it isn't totally normal, that's all. Your father and I support you and your choices in boyfriends."

"We're not dating, Mom!" Nadia claimed.

Anabella shook her head and looked over at her sister. She had started a bad spiral of events and needed to back out of this. "Mom, what about now, the mafia in New York? Those wives all marry knowing what they are getting into."

"Yes, but that's different. You kids aren't mafia brats."

"No, they're just Mavericks," William chimed in. "Let's drop this. We can all agree to disagree about whether women are attracted to bad boys, but in this case, the apples don't fall from the tree." He gave Laura a sharp look and then a grin. Whatever that had meant to their mother, it caused her to stop arguing. Anabella and Nadia both looked at each other and smiled. She knew that she and her sister would soon have to have a long talk with their mother.

Thinking back on the whole event, she realized that she had probably overreacted and should have cooled her engines a bit, but everyone knew that once the Mavericks got revved up, there was no stopping them.

There was a ding of the elevator door, and she saw Carter signaling her to step on. She hadn't realized that she was off in a dazed dream state while waiting to go up to their room.

"You okay there, mia bella?"

"Yeah, I was just thinking about stuff. No worries, babe." She gave him a kiss on the cheek as she walked past him and stepped into the elevator. The noise the elevator doors made when they closed made Anabella feel slightly bad for thinking ill of Carlisle at one point. She looked over at Carter and realized her mom really was right. The bad boys were always the ones women secretly wanted.

The resort suite that Carter and Carlisle had booked for them was top of the line. Carter made sure that each nuance had been thought about and taken care of. One thing he was good at was attention to detail. He had initially wanted this to be just a vacation with Anabella alone, but in the end he'd decided that they would have more fun with her sister and Carlisle. He and Carlisle hadn't vacationed much together. Occasionally, they would take a job together that would send them out to a remote tropical locale, but they only ever stayed an extra day or so. Carlisle hadn't been big on vacations until he'd gotten with Nadia.

Carter realized what they said was true; everything changed when you got married. That thought made him wonder what would change about him and Anabella if she accepted his impending proposal. Hopefully all that changed for them was where she laid her head every night, on his pillow.

"You look deep in thought there. The dinner menu cannot be that complicated, Carter." Anabella smiled at him. Her teeth shimmered in the sunlight as it traveled through their open window.

He had promised her dinner alone tonight. The truth was, it wasn't a necessary promise. He and Carlisle had already decided that most of the dinners would be alone, except for the surprise they had planned for the murder mystery theater.

"I am trying to decide between steak and fish."

"What is there to decide on? Steak!" Anabella said with excitement.

"You can get amazing steak back in Texas. I'm just thinking about the fish. Cameroon is right on the coast of the Atlantic Ocean. Imagine how good fresh fish would taste without all the waste and pollution back home."

She waved him off. "Fish is fish. It's smelly and gamey. Steak is, well, steak. It's what's for dinner." She grinned at him.

"Are you a walking commercial now?"

"I could be. What am I advertising?"

"How about something succulent, tender, and juicy?" The look in his eye said hunger in every way possible. He knew she knew exactly what was on his mind.

"Oh my..."

He stood up from the table and set the menu aside. With a few strides, he closed any distance that was between them and swept her into his arms. With a smile and wink, he leaned in and captured her lips. She tasted of honey and cinnamon. That made him wonder what she had just eaten. Carter ran his tongue over her teeth and she slowly opened her mouth for them.

Their embrace felt powerful to him. Everything about her was overwhelming. This must have been why Ivy always cautioned him against women, because once he was hooked, he was a goner. "We can have steak, if that's what you want, mia bella."

"I love when you call me that."

"Good."

"But you never told me why you nicknamed me that. You know in Italian it means beautiful, right?"

He shook his head. "Technically you are correct, but the original meaning, actually the literal translation in Latin, means war."

"And why do you call me that?" Anabella said in a quizzical tone.

"Maybe you create a war inside me," he said coolly.

"Do I?" she teased.

He shook his head from side to side and grew serious. "No. It's just short for Anabella, and it is pretty."

Anabella laughed, and her smile went from ear to ear. "I think I'd rather stir a war inside of you than be called something pretty." She lifted her hands in the air to signal air quotes at that last word.

"See, that's why we are a pair. We both love the finer things in life, like a good war."

Carter watched Anabella pick up the menu and look it over it. "Sides?"

"Salad, soup?"

"Both?"

"Perfect."

Carter walked over to the telephone that was mounted to the wall on the balcony and pressed zero.

"Thank you for calling the front desk, Mr. Jackson. What can I do for you tonight?"

"We would like room service please. Two steaks, medium rare, two house salads, two cups of your soup of the day, two waters, and two iced teas. Oh, and please send up chocolate covered strawberries and a bottle of champagne."

"Very good, sir. We will have that up to you in the next forty-five minutes."

"There is an extra twenty in it for the server if you can get it here in twenty minutes or less."

"Yes, sir."

The line went blank, and he set the receiver down on the base of the telephone. Cater looked over at Anabella and said, "Food will be here shortly. Do you want to rent a movie for tonight, or shall we enjoy the sunset on the balcony?"

"The balcony is nice. I love the weather here. It isn't that horrid humidity of Houston, but it is still nice and warm."

"It's more of a dry heat, and it takes time to get used to, for natives of Texas that is." He gave her a nod and watched her turn her head to look at the horizon. "Isn't the sunset perfect?"

"The colors look so vivid."

"You can't find such a magical night in the States." He pulled Anabella close and wrapped his arms around her.

"What a pity. I wish Mom and Dad were here to see this. They would love it."

"I'm sure William and Laura have seen evenings this beautiful. They have traveled to a lot of places."

"Probably. Good point."

"You're not missing your family already, are you? The adventure has just begun."

"It's not that I'm missing them; it's that sometimes I just wish I could share it with all of the ones I love."

CHAPTER THREE

"Nadia!" Anabella shouted as she watched her sister jump from the tree out into the open and grab the long green vine hanging from the adjacent branch. "You're going to kill yourself, and then Mom and Dad will skin me alive!"

"Stop your worrying. You know you are going to do it too."

She watched Nadia glide down to the ground, and she felt her heartbeat suddenly begin to slow down at the knowledge that Nadia was now safe. "I am not. I am going to stay right here, pull my phone out, and call Carter."

"What is Carter going to do?"

Looking out across the scene, Anabella felt her throat gulp. "I don't know, but it's better than jumping to my death."

"What happened to that military sense of adventure you once had?" Nadia looked back up at her sister as she planted her feet firmly on the ground after sliding down the vine for about a hundred feet. She continued to yell, "I hadn't realized you'd become a chicken."

Anabella rolled her eyes and shook her head. "I won't fall for that, Nadia. I grew up and realized it was act of God that I hadn't broken a bone, or worse, my neck, with all that stuff I did before." She looked at the screen of her iPhone and clicked on the little round button at the bottom. "Siri, call Carter."

"Calling Carter," the automatic voice replied back.

She placed the phone to her ear and waited in silence. The only noise her mind was focusing on was the sound of her heart beating loudly through her chest.

"Hey, mia bella." His voice was smooth and seductive even when he was simply saying hello to her. She couldn't stop herself from smiling. He always had a way with her mind when he spoke, as if he was a hypnotic drug that kept her from seeing anything else around her.

"Carter, I have a problem."

She heard his deep laughter coming from her iPhone. "As if Carlisle and I expected anything less to happen, sending you and Nadia off together."

"No, this time I did it. I'm stuck."

"Where are you stuck?"

She looked around as if she was looking for a marker of some kind that she could give him as a guidepost to find her. "In a tree..." She let her voice trail off, waiting for his reply.

"A tree. My, your descriptive use of words is overpowering, mia bella. I can see why Nadia is the one who received the gift of writing."

"Don't make fun of me. Just have Carlisle track Nadia's phone and bring something to get me out of the tree. It's about one hundred feet up."

"No comment. I'll have Carlisle turn on the tracker, but this just goes to show you two women need men. You were not built for independence."

"I am not going to dignify that with an answer. See you soon."

Anabella slipped her phone back into her pocket once the call ended, and she looked back down towards her sister. "This isn't going to help me at all with him, is it?" She could see Nadia shrugging from up in the tree. She couldn't help sighing. She didn't know what had come over her and her adventurous side, but she really didn't want to plummet to her death.

"I think it will be okay. He probably likes being the knight in shining armor. I mean, he is a man, after all."

Anabella sat down on the thick limb of the tree and attempted to make herself as comfortable as she could. The bark felt hard and rough under her body as she applied more pressure to it with her back nestled against the ninety degree angle of the limb and tree trunk.

"Hey, Nadia?" she said.

"Yeah, Ana?"

"Remind me why we came to Africa."

"Because you wanted to see a real lion not in a zoo but in its natural habitat. Why?"

"'Cause I think we can go home now, mission accomplished." Anabella lifted her arm and pointed her fingers out in front of herself. She guessed it to be two football fields away, but she could see the yellow mane glistening in the sunlight.

"Oh my god!" she heard her sister scream. She looked down to see Nadia trying to climb back up the tree.

"What are you doing? It's a cat. They can climb trees!" she called down to Nadia.

"I'd rather be in a freaking tree than sitting on the ground waiting to be kitty food!"

"We aren't safe in either place! Jump down; I'm coming down."

"Oh?" Nadia looked up and couldn't help laughing. "Now you're not too scared?"

"It just got real! Now be quiet. We don't want to attract him," Anabella said with fierce emotion in her voice.

Anabella looked at the green vine hanging before her, and she knew her options were limited to that. She turned her head back in the direction of the lion, where the yellow mane was still visible. She got to her feet and balanced herself on the thick limb. *You can do this, you can do this*, she thought to herself. With an oomph, she pushed off the limb. She soared into the air and reached out to the vine. After a quick second of hang time, her arms were now securely wrapped around the vine, and she began to slide down the hundred feet to the ground.

"Hey, you made it down!" she heard Carter say as he and Carlisle walked up through the trees behind them.

"Shhh," Nadia and Anabella both said at the same time.

Anabella walked over to Carter, wrapped her arms around his waist, and held him close. She leaned into his ear and whispered, "There is a lion about two hundred yards away. We have to get out of here, now." She felt some relief when he wrapped his arms around her shoulders in a protective manner, but they all knew it without saying anything. They had to get out of there.

Carter looked at the Maverick sisters and wasn't surprised in the least that this had happened. In fact, he and Carlisle had a bet going on that they couldn't last twenty-four hours without having to call for help. Carlisle was deeply in love, and he used that to his advantage. He couldn't see Nadia's flaws, one which consisted of putting his woman in danger on a daily basis. On their way to rescue the girls, Carter had collected on his hundred dollar bet. It felt good to be needed, needed by someone other than a society who had to have individuals like him and Carlisle around to keep the balance of good and evil in check.

He had his arms wrapped around Anabella now. She felt warm even in the blazing sun of Africa. There had been much debate over bringing them to this continent, but at the end of the day, these two girls would do whatever they wanted. He and Carlisle were simply along for the ride and to keep them safe, or so their father had said the night before they flew out.

"We have a jeep over there." He pointed behind him towards the direction the two of them had walked up in. "I'm sure we can out drive the lion. Let's go back to the jeep."

"Thank God. Let's go," he heard Nadia say to Carlisle as they all turned in the direction of the jeep and began to walk towards it.

"What had you girls been doing to get yourself stuck in a tree, mia bella?"

"Don't ask," she replied quickly.

Nadia made a noise and then quickly stopped talking when Anabella shot an evil glance over her shoulder. Something had certainly been going on before they called them, and he was going to find out. They had been tasked with keeping the two women safe, and that was a full-time job, especially with Nadia around. She was a walking drama magnet, and everyone around her was always subject to insanity at any moment when the unknown was presented to Mrs. Ali.

Mrs. Ali. It still seemed like yesterday that the Mavericks and Carlisle were at his house in Houston for the wedding. He was happy for his brother-in-arms, but he still couldn't believe what had taken place, a man of Mr. A's history and reputation finding love. It hadn't been through a dating site at least, but still attached to the internet somehow. He had never been the Casanova of their small group of friends. That had always been Carter's title, a title he had recently hung up on the wall for another man to wear with pride. Most likely, it would be Tavin next, he thought.

From what he knew of Tavin, he was a ladies' man. He was good looking and an intelligent man. Then again, those were two requirements for being part of the brotherhood. Overall, Tavin was a young man who had a lot of potential for greatness; he just needed a few more years of maturing. Men always developed a bit slower than expected, or at least that's what Ivy always told him.

This had never been an occupation that warranted a wife or girlfriend, but as the times changed, he realized their needs had changed too. The need to come home to a safe place, a safe woman, had begun to outweigh the need to not be tied down.

"Carter," he heard Anabella say as she snapped her fingers in front of his face. "Yo, Carter," she said again.

"Yeah?" he questioned.

"You spaced out on us. We just wanted to make sure you were still in the present mind."

"I was just thinking about something, nothing big. Come on, we are almost to the jeep."

The blue and black vehicle started to show up in the near distance ahead, and the girls broke out into a run and headed for it. He heard Carlisle pull the keys from his pocket. Their little jingling noise was easy to detect among the many sounds he was now hearing in this outback atmosphere.

"Hey, the jeep's waiting. Come on, guys!" Nadia yelled.

The two of them shot a quick glance to one another, and then both of them broke out into a run and quickly got into the vehicle.

Once they were on their way, he could feel the tension among the four of them lessen. The immediate threat to their lives was now far away, and the space between them was growing greater with each second.

"I guess you were right. We do need a tracker on us at all times."

"It is good to hear you come to your senses, wife."

"Well, husband, not everything is one of your cases or conspiracy theories."

"No, but your safety is always a top priority. The only thing that scares me more than the idea of having to retire to a white picket fence house and never traveling again is the idea of Kain and your father coming after me for letting you get lost, or worse, hurt!"

Everyone in the jeep erupted in laughter. That was a true statement. After the wedding at Carter's home, their father and brother had sat Carlisle down, and Carter of course had been within earshot as the two Maverick men told Carlisle exactly what would happen to him if anything happened to their baby girl. Then they had shot him a look, knowing he had heard everything and simply said, "You too." It was the happiest moment Carter's house had seen to date. Real love, unconditional love, that's what the Mavericks had for each and every member of their family.

"After the lion danger, do you guys want to go back to the resort?" He looked up into the rear view mirror and saw the sisters look at each other and smile. He and Carlisle had learned a while ago that, when they smiled like that, it was likely a scary moment for one or both of the sister's male companions.

"Yes," Carlisle said firmly before either woman could speak.

"No!" they both said in unison.

"Yes," Carter repeated. "We have dinner plans that Carlisle and I would like to make it to today."

"Who needs dinner when you have us to feast on?" Nadia said playfully.

"You will like these dinner plans, Nadia," Carlisle said to her. "I made them with you in mind specifically."

"Oh lord help us. Someone's going to end up hurt!" Anabella teased.

"Now, Ana, you know it's not always my fault. Stop making it seem like I am the one who takes all the attention. If I remember right, the tree climbing just now was all you."

"You can't prove that."

Nadia laughed nodding her head. "Oh yeah I can. I just don't have the energy."

"Girls, come on. Just trust us, okay? Carlisle planned a fun night. I promise."

With that, they all sat silently as they went back to the resort. The scenery looked beautiful. Magnetic and peaceful, the colors flourished under the sun, and the grass swayed in a wave sort of motion as the jeep drove past. There were trees off in the distance that looked like they reached high into the atmosphere. Everything was extensive and never-ending. There were even flocks of birds flying through the air, making peaceful noises as they passed.

The resort Carlisle had booked reminded Nadia of the Taj Mahal in Atlantic City. She had gone there on an assignment five years ago and had always wanted to go back. As they approached the entrance, the streets were lined with white and gold colored cylinders. The rooms they had each checked into had been decorated with a deep green coloring accenting the white walls. The eggshell colored sheets were made of Egyptian cotton, and the comforter on each bed had the softest texture she had felt before.

Each room had an enclosed flat screen television where with the push of a button, the television receded from the room to be hidden behind the drop down layer of protection that blended into the wall. Carlisle had told Carter than when Nadia had found out the price of the room per night, she'd blown a gasket. Carter wished he had been around to see that.

They were lucky to have found a suite available on short notice. Theirs consisted of two bedrooms that were connected by a shared kitchen and living room space. They had quickly discovered after their trip during spring break, that the girls were easier to manage if they stayed together in close quarters.

Carter had been around for a year now. A lot had happened since November of 2013. After Carlisle and Nadia's wedding he and Anabella had casually dated for a while. He had flown her down to Houston every other weekend, and when she wasn't in Houston, he'd flown up to Cedar Rapids. They had quickly become comfortable with one another. Neither of them had been looking for a serious relationship though. Anabella's reserve unit had had talks of being called up to go to a mission in the Middle East. Carter rarely pulled strings, but he had that time. Anabella didn't know that. She just assumed some bureaucratic reason had stopped her from leaving with her friends, and that was fine by him.

Carlisle had told him the Maverick family was like a drug, and he'd better stay far away if he didn't want to get addicted. That had been at the Christmas celebration shortly after their wedding. Obviously he'd ignored the warning, and even now the two nephews were under his skin.

Their family had just suffered a loss of sorts. Kain's divorce had finally become legal. Anabella and Nadia seemed excited she was finally out of their lives. Laura and William seemed more concerned. Carter was still forming opinions of Anabella's parents, and it gave him some reassurance that they weren't quick to send a spouse packing, no matter what the situation.

The boys, Leon and Daman, seemed to be coping well. Anabella and Nadia had made it clear that since the divorce they wanted to stay close to home for Kain and the children's sake. That was part of the reason this trip had been planned, to give everyone a break.

And Carter was glad that he had.

"Carter?" Anabella said as she walked into their adjoining room.

"Yeah?" His tone mimicked the soft one she had just given, as if speaking was almost forbidden.

"You looked really deep in thought. Everything okay?"

He nodded his head and looked over at her. "I've just been thinking about the last year."

"Oh? What about it?"

"How much chaos you have brought into my world. Carlisle was right about you Mavericks."

"Now I don't know that that is fair. You and Carlisle cause quite a bit of drama yourselves when you are working."

That made Carter laugh a rich, deep laugh. "That's different kind of drama."

Anabella shrugged her shoulders. "Either way, you two give us a run for our money any day of the week!"

He walked over to the dresser, pulled a drawer open, and took out the green and white top she brought along for the trip. This one was his favorite. It accented her skin perfectly, and it showed just enough cleavage to make every man in the room jealous but not enough to make him jealous at the attention she pulled. "Will you wear this one for me tonight? I think it will help with our dinner plans."

She cocked an eyebrow at him and tilted her head. "Whatever you say, but now I am curious as to what kind of dinner we are going to have."

"Just wait and see. I promise you will enjoy it."

"I am sure I will. Do you have a pant selection?"

"Your black skirt, the one with the slit."

"I really hope I don't have to do any running tonight. It is safe to say that isn't going to be happening in this outfit you've planned."

Carter shook his head and handed her the top. "No, ma'am. I promise tonight you won't have to do any running."

She took the top from him and placed a soft kiss on his cheek. "Okay, holding you to that."

CHAPTER FOUR

Carlisle looked over Nadia's hands as they sat down on their bed. She had received some type of rope burn as she'd slid down the vine earlier. He had brought some balm out of his suitcase that he always carried with him to try and ease her burn.

"Why didn't you say anything earlier?" he asked her.

"I didn't want anyone to know. I get teased enough as it is."

"Well, I will fix it, have no fear."

Nadia smiled up at him as he ran his cool fingers over her warm palm while lightly applying the balm he had stored in his knapsack.

"So tonight is a murder mystery dinner," he told her. He kept his eyes fixed on hers as he watched her excitement display along her face. "There is going to be a side bet going on which couple can figure out who the killer is first, but I know something they don't know."

She sat silently, grinning and listening.

"We're going to be the killers."

"That's going to be awesome! And Carter doesn't know?"

He shook his head. "I want us to have a lot of fun tonight. The director already said he would let me pick our form of killing and who the victim is going to be."

She rubbed her hands together pushing more of the balm into her skin. The glint on her eye almost looked evil and fun all twisted into one. "They are never going to see us coming!"

"Nope, and that is the point of it, to keep them guessing. So, Mrs. Ali, if you had any way to kill someone, what would it be?" He loved how her smile curved up her face whenever he called her by his last name. Women were so funny about that. Names. Some loved taking their husband's, others loathed it. He felt lucky that Nadia loved him enough to want to be branded with his name and everything that came along with that.

"Do I really have to pick now? I want to think on it! I mean, imagine, with my hands, the power. Or, oh wait! What if I'm attacked and it is self-defense? I could..." Nadia's voice trailed off as she started thinking of all of the possibilities. Carlisle watched her pace the room, looking in the mirror as she walked by, trying on different shirts. It seemed she wanted to look just the part.

"Nadia, I think you are overthinking this." He walked over, placed his hands on her shoulders, and made her look at him in the eyes. "The point of this is fun. I'm going to count to three and the first thing you say when I say three is what you will use." He waited a moment to get her to calm down. "One ... two ... three."

"Planter!"

Carlisle turned his head to see the planter next to the television that contained ivy. He looked back at Nadia and started to chuckle. "I see originality will be the name of this game!"

"It will be like our own live version of clue, but in Africa!"

"Yes, and you have to remember not to give yourself away. You know how you get, all excited and cute."

"You think I'm cute?" she playfully flirted.

Carlisle walked up behind her and wrapped his arms around her waist. "Not just cute, adorable." He lightly kissed the top of her head and then brought his hand over her bottom and spanked her. "Now chop-chop, get dressed so we can get to it."

"Do you think there will be dinner with this murder?"

"Sure, if you want there to be. I think the longer we pull it out before the person is offed, the better."

"Are we going to have to give some special sign when we are ready?"

Carlisle nodded in affirmation. "Yes. The person that I spoke with when I reserved our dinner said they will give one of us a special button, and whenever we are ready for the murder to take place, we simply press the button and the lights will go out. Then we do what we gotta do to make it seem like someone has died."

"Will the person know to play along?"

"I am sure they will." He walked over to the closet and pulled out his formal evening attire and began to dress. "If it is anything like the ones back in the States, they will take us all aside individually so no one is excluded and explain the rules to us and then seat us to dinner."

"I've always wanted to do one of these, and now I finally get to."

Carlisle watched Nadia as she continued to get dressed up. He loved her neckline and her smile. Hell he loved everything about her. He couldn't help thinking about her constantly and thanking his gods daily for her.

He and Carter had talked about Nadia and Anabella quite a few times over the last year. Carter was getting hooked into the Maverick family. He didn't want his friend to shy away from his upbeat and vivacious sister-in-law. He simply wanted him to slow down, not that that had ever stopped Carlisle when he was pursuing Nadia.

"Do you think Anabella is as into Carter as he is into her?" Carlisle asked his wife.

She looked over her shoulder at him with a slight surprised expression. "You don't think she is?"

"Not sure. She is having fun, but I was just thinking about them, and us."

"Wanting to make sure your bff isn't hurt?" Nadia said slightly teasingly.

"I don't think Ana is going to hurt him intentionally, but maybe yes, trying to make sure my 'bff' isn't hurt."

"Ana enjoys him, and she enjoys all of our adventures, of that I can assure you. She hasn't had this much fun since she was in the military.

So I think they are both good for each other and fools if they don't clearly see that."

"I wasn't saying they don't see it. I worry for your father, having two men like us with his daughters."

"Trust me, William loves you two. He knows we are safer now than we ever have been."

"If we ever have a daughter, she will not be bringing home a guy like us."

Nadia laughed and nodded her head. "I can agree to that." Then she walked over and wrapped her arms around Carlisle's neck. "Daughter, huh? We haven't really talked about kids."

He shrugged. "It is always a possibility, right?" He noticed something change in her facial expression and wondered if it was the conversation about potential kids or her palm bothering her.

She nodded in agreement. "Yes, good thing Mom wasn't here for this comment, or she would start bouncing up and down with joy."

"Your mother is almost as bad as your nephew."

"Our nephews. They are yours now too, remember."

"Yes, yes, our nephews." He leaned in and kissed her on the lips and then turned her away from him and gave her a slight push. "Finish getting ready. We are due down there in an a little under thirty minutes."

It didn't take them much longer to finish getting ready, and as they moved into their shared living room area, they saw Carter and Anabella waiting for them. Nadia smiled, thinking about the conversation she had previously had with Carlisle, both about the dinner and about her sister's happiness, and that made her happy. She wanted all of her family to be as happy as she was, and she knew it was only a matter of time before they even had a new woman for Kain.

"You look hot, Ana," Nadia said. She gave her sister the once over and then did a motion with her finger for her to spin around. Anabella was dressed in a green top, perfect for dinner and a black skirt that flowed down her long legs and slightly dragged the ground. She had on their grandmother's diamond earrings and matching necklace. She looked fantastic.

Carter, on the other hand, looked out of his league. While he was still dressed in a suit, it wasn't as classy as Anabella's dress was. Or maybe it was simply because everyone was used to seeing Carter dressed up, so it didn't come to a surprise to them. His tie, however, did match her top perfectly, and the handkerchief in his breast pocket did as well.

Nadia looked over at Carlisle and frowned. "Why do I feel like we are suddenly very under dressed for tonight's festivities?"

"Because it seems we are, my pet. Don't worry though. Everyone will just have to deal with our attire."

"Nadia, you don't look bad! You look cute," Anabella said as she walked over to her sister and wrapped an arm around her. "I'm older, so I have to dress fancier to keep the boys' attention, you see." She wiggled her eyebrows in Carter's direction. Nadia watched him completely ignore her comment and continue about his business with the brandy decanter on the bar.

"Well, I am glad you think I look cute. I'll just have you walk on one end and the guys can walk in between us, that way no one sees us right next to each other."

Carter walked up beside them and chuckled. "Nadia you are putting way too much effort into this. You are overthinking."

"That's what she does," Carlisle joined in saying.

"Well, I can see this is quickly turning into a 'let's pick on Nadia' party, so let's get down to dinner, yeah? I'm starved."

The four of them made their way to the dining room, and as they entered, their breaths were taken away. The setting was immaculate. Upon first entry, off to the right, they could see the area that was set up as the dining room. Then, as they followed the wall around from right to left, they saw several other rooms. There was a library, two bedrooms, a kitchen, and a living room. There were backdrops along each room to help people visualize the house they were supposed to be staying in, and objects were set across all of the rooms that could either be used as the murder weapon or used to help solve the case.

The library held a display of magnifying glasses not just one but several and several different types of them too, not just the traditional looking circular devices. Nadia began to step towards the living room mock up area when the door opened and more people began to come inside. Everyone took a quick glance at one another and began to introduce themselves.

There was the typical guy from accounting, Steve. Then an older gentleman named Jason from the United Kingdom. Of course there was the single mother, Donna, and her partner for the time being, Casey. Then finally there were Charles and Oliver, brothers who were on vacation together, they said.

Something caused Nadia to get a weird sensation in the pit of her stomach. There was something off about these people, maybe not all of them, but one or two of them for sure.

Just before Nadia could start doing what she did best, investigating, the hosts for tonight's event stepped inside and welcomed all of them.

"Ladies and gentleman, my name is Gerardo, and I will be your host for tonight." His deep voice echoed throughout the room. "We will start dinner off with a four course meal. The soup is a specialty from our chef's home town and is followed by a salad of your choice. The main course will be a vegetable medley accompanying a specialty of the hotel, giraffe meat. And for dessert, we will be having a very special bread pudding that our award winning chef has had featured on the Today Show when they were visiting Africa last year."

Nadia noticed everyone's expressions when he mentioned that they would be dining on giraffe meat. She had never tasted anything exotic before but was confident that Mr. A and Mr. J had both had the luxury of fine dining when they were off on their travels. She turned to Anabella and smiled. "Won't this be exciting?!"

With a quick nod full of her own excitement, Anabella was fast to reply, "Oh yes, Mom and Dad have told me how much they love giraffe. Now Kain will be the odd man out for once!"

Both sisters laughed, and the guys turned their heads simultaneously, looking in their direction. They had learned quickly that it was best to avoid the Maverick girls when their laughter started like that.

"Poor Kain, always missing out. We should call him after dinner."

"What time will it be back home?" Nadia asked.

"No idea, but does it matter? You know he will take our call day or night, or so he claims."

"Girls," Carter said, "listen to the host. You're being rude."

Both sisters gave a "Sorry" in reply and re-focused their attention on the man who was giving them directions.

"As I was saying, you will each walk into the dining room area and sit down at your place cards. You will have the waiters and waitresses serving you, and you have my word, they will not be your killer!"

There was an audible sound that came from the crowd as he emphasized the word "killer."

"We have already been in touch with your villain of this evening, and I can assure you, you are standing beside him or her right now!"

Everyone turned their heads and suspiciously looked at one another. The questionable stares started, and it was easy to see in each of the participants' minds they were sizing everyone up, seeing who their biggest threat was.

"All we ask of you is to not physically harm one another. What I mean by this is, in the heat of the moment, remember, you are not actually going to punch the killer out if you get into a fight. You simply give the command to the police officer, who will be played by my assistant, Toby."

The heads of all the participants turned to the left as the doors opened and a young man, probably about twenty-five, walked into the room wearing an old fashioned 1800's English police officer's uniform.

He bowed his head and then everyone turned their attention back to Gerardo.

"Toby does not know who the killer is, so you must convince him. Come up with your evidence, and he will interrogate the suspect just as if it was real life. Now, each of you will be given a black box with a button. In the event you need to be pulled from the game for any reason, be it for your health or the game simply gets too intense, you push the button and the lights will all come back on to the level they are now, and you will be escorted out. One of your black boxes is actually a light dimmer. When that person, who is your killer, pushes it, it will go pitch black for fifteen seconds. Enough time for you to place your hand on your victim's head signaling them to pass out and play dead."

"Are there any questions?"

The room was silent for a moment, and then someone spoke. "When do we get our boxes?"

"They have already been placed on your seat at the dining table. You must not change seats as it will affect the whole game."

Gerardo paused for a few moments and then clapped his hands together quickly four times and the lights began to fade. "Please be seated, ladies and gentleman. It is time."

Everyone walked to the dining room very quietly and slowly. It was obvious they were all taking in one another's presence and demeanor. Since Nadia had been with Carlisle, he had been working with her on not showing her weakness on her face. She was aware she always had a tell, and she was now nervous that Carter and Anabella would pick up on that. She tried to divert her mind to anything and everything else to keep attention focused on the four course meal.

Carlisle pulled out a chair and gestured to Nadia to have a seat. As she sat, she noticed that the chair cushion was extremely soft. The dishes on the table were obviously expensive china. They shimmered in the light, even with it so low. She looked around as Carlisle sat to her right to take notice of everyone's positioning. Who was she going to choose as her first victim, and when?

Two doors behind Nadia and Carlisle opened up, and five waiters and five waitresses walked out, all carrying dishes. They each aligned themselves behind one of the guests, and at the same time, they all leaned forward and set the soup down at the tables. A round soup bowl sat right in the middle of the plate that rested on each of their spots.

Then, as if an army sergeant had yelled a command, they all turned and marched back into the two doors.

"Wow that was intense," Nadia whispered to Carlisle.

"My pet, it has just started. Wait until the murder happens."

"You are really excited about that, aren't you?"

All he could do was look at her and grin, and she knew his thoughts.

"Hey, Mr. A," Anabella's slightly elevated voice said from across the room.

"Yes, dear sister-in-law?"

"My money is on you. I bet you solve this crime before we have a chance to finish this elegant dinner."

Nadia reached to take a sip of her water and choked as she heard her sister's words. Well, technically he had already solved it, but she didn't want everyone knowing that.

"Ana, I'm on vacation. I will let someone else do all the leg work this time."

The accountant, Steve, quickly chimed in. "You a detective back home?"

The room was silent as everyone waited for Carlisle to answer him.

"Something like that."

CHAPTER FIVE

The dinner started out deliciously in Anabella's opinion. The warm liquid slid down her throat, making her purr out in pleased approval. She hadn't realized how hungry she was until the food touched her palate. Today had been full of excitement and adventure, so much so that neither she nor Nadia had really taken the time to eat, and that hadn't even been noticed until exactly forty seconds ago.

She had been seated next to Charles and Casey. She wasn't entirely sure why she and Carter had been split up, but she supposed she would be okay with it for a meal. It wasn't like they weren't sharing a room or anything. They had plenty of time together. One thing that she had grown to really like about Carter was the fact that his easy nature was infectious, and it seemed anything they did together always turned out okay because he was never in a mood of disappointment.

Never before had she met a man like this. Even Mr. A, as cool and laid back as he was, needed to have his way. She began to watch Carter as he interacted with Donna. That woman was going to be trouble. She was already flirting with Carter, and right in front of her date too. Clearly a hussy, no doubt.

"Excuse me?" Anabella said in the direction Carter sat. "Would you mind passing the salt? I could use a tad more flavor in my soup."

"Of course, Ana. Do you need anything else, darling?" The way he said "darling" sounded odd. It wasn't in his usual tenor, and it seemed as if he was emphasizing something for no purpose at all. Maybe he was detecting her slight jealousy at watching him and the other woman talk about something pointless.

"No, honey, that's quite alright." Anabella's eyes drifted around the table and landed on her sister's, which were staring back at her in shock. Yes, she knew she was acting weird, but Nadia acted weird on a constant and daily basis. She would just get over it.

"Casey, what is it you do for a living?" she heard Carter ask.

"I'm in sales," was all he said. Quite the talker he wasn't.

"Like car sales?" Nadia asked. Anabella laughed under her breath at that comment. Leave it to Nadia to be tacky in front of new people.

"Direct sales," he replied.

"What's that?" Anabella chimed in with.

"You know, door to door?" He looked at the two sisters like they were dumb, as if everyone should know exactly what direct sales meant.

"The type of salesman we avoid, my pet," Carlisle said not so quietly under his breath.

Casey gave Carlisle an almost evil glare and then turned his attention back to finishing his soup. Tonight's game was starting out very heated already. Anabella couldn't wait until someone was murdered and then all the real fun would begin.

Shortly after everyone was finished eating, the wait staff came in, removed the first round, and brought out the second course. The salad looked delicious. Anabella selected the cobb, while her sister and Carlisle picked a wedge. Carter went on the adventurous side and picked the traditional African salad, whatever that was. It all looked like lettuce to Anabella, and it tasted fabulous. By the time they were ready for the third course, Anabella had begun to wish she had been seated properly by Carter. She didn't think it would be an issue asking someone to move.

"Casey, would it trouble you any to switch seats with me so I could sit next to Carter?" she asked in as sweet and nice of a tone as possible. She noticed that Casey first looked to Carter as if asking if this was something he wished for too.

After a nod, he pushed his chair back and stood up, picking up his cup of water and glass of wine and began to move towards Anabella's chair. She had pushed her chair back and mimicked his actions as she took her new seat next to Carter. There was a bit of silverware exchanging before the two people had settled completely back in their seats.

"All better?" Carter asked as he placed his hand on top of Anabella's as she finished placing her fork on the table.

"Quite. Now I'm next to the sexiest man in the room."

She heard Carlisle clear his throat, and both sisters began chuckling at the same time. Carter and Carlisle shot each other a friendly glance, and then everyone went on about their business, talking among themselves.

Anabella felt Carter's hair scrape past her ears and then suddenly felt his lips press into her neck. The kiss startled her for a second, and then she calmed when he began whispering to her. "You have no idea how pretty you are tonight, Anabella. I am the luckiest man here."

Before Anabella could respond with a flirtatious remark, the lights went out. Her heart began to beat rapidly. She knew it was only a matter of time before they came back on and one of their dinner mates would be removed from the game. She didn't want to be that one person chosen. Not yet.

There was a loud crash that came from the right of Anabella. Slowly, the lights began to come back on, and she saw Casey lying in his meal. His head was resting on his plate with a planter placed on top of it. She smiled when she looked over at Carter and saw he was still standing and not pretending to be dead. Then she looked over at Nadia and Mr. A. Her family was all there, and now the real fun would begin.

"So do we just start guessing who the killer is?" Charles asked.

"No, we start playing Sherlock Holmes," Donna responded.

"And what would Holmes do?" Charles retorted in a snippy tone.

"He would analyze the evidence," Carlisle said.

Carter had seen his pseudo sister-in-law race around the table and pretend to smash the planter on Casey's head. He was sure that Carlisle remembered his training in the Army Rangers for night vision tactics. They had done over a thousand hours of training in the pitch black. Sometimes he even thought that his vision was better in the dark exposed to no light than it was during the day with the lights on, but now this posed a new dilemma for him. Should he use this knowledge that he had to his advantage and solve the case quickly, or should he help Nadia out and sway the others to a different villain, and was Carlisle in on her doing the killing, he wondered.

A planter did not seem like the weapon of choice for Carlisle, but it was Nadia carrying out the task of killing and not him. A plant pot did seem like the perfect desperate housewife weapon, something that most women now days had around and something that a man didn't find threatening.

In the end, he decided it would be more fun to keep the fact to himself, hold back, and let the others take a crack at solving the mystery.

"First we should get fingerprints!" Anabella called out.

"Shouldn't we take photographs of the crime scene first in case we move or change anything later on?" Donna questioned Anabella with.

Carter watched her shrug her shoulders, then looked between Carter and Carlisle for what he assumed was their suggestion.

"We could take photos and then fingerprints, but you know that would only work if the person's prints were in the data base. Since we don't have a database handy, you would have to take all of our prints, and that is against the law. You don't have legal authority in this case so far to take them, even just hypothetically."

The room let out an audible grumble as the people realized that Carlisle was most likely correct, even though Carter believed a good officer could argue probable cause since there weren't a lot of people in the room and it was obvious one of them performed the murderer. It would be a good reason to compel someone to give their prints.

Or someone could simply lift the prints off of the dinner utensils. Should he mention that to Añabella? He was in the middle of debating in his mind when an idea struck him. He could mess with Nadia, do a little role reversal of the bad guy, and use the information for bribery instead.

That's what he was going to do.

"I think we should split into pairs," Carter announced.

"Great idea!" Anabella quickly chimed in, wrapping her arm around his and smiling up at him.

"Not so fast with those accolades. I don't think you will like my next suggestion."

"What do you have in mind, brother?" Carlisle asked while giving him a very pointed look.

"I think we should split into new teams, not with the person we came with, to help sharpen our senses and work on building teams."

No one seemed to like that idea at first, so he made a slight adjustment. "Okay, how about not your date but you could do someone in your party? For instance, Anabella would go with Carlisle, and I would go with Nadia."

"I'm okay with that," Anabella said.

"Me too," Donna agreed.

Slowly, everyone agreed, and together they came into a new partnership. Steve was the only one without a partner, and after standing around for a minute, looking at everyone, he walked over to Charles and Donna and asked if he could join them.

Once everyone was paired off in their groups, they started working, discussing the details of the case that they could see. Carter heard the murmurs and whispers that took place, and he had to try and stop himself from laughing at the different comments he heard.

Nadia touched his arm and pointed towards the fake dead body. "Don't you want to go thoroughly check it out?"

"No need."

"No need?" she repeated with a questioning tone.

"That's right, I know who did it."

He watched her face take on a shocked expression for a moment, and then she regained her composure enough to ask, "You do?"

With a single nod, he gave a quick reply. "You."

A nervous giggle came out of her mouth, and that made him smile. He could understand why Carlisle had fallen for her so easily. The Maverick sisters had quite a few little habits that made them so endearing.

"Your Mr. A hasn't trained you well enough to hold your poker face, but I'm not sure what I want to do with this information exactly," he said in a low tone.

"It's not me." She shook her head profusely back and forth.

"Little pseudo sister, yes it is. Now let me decide how I shall play this." He tapped the tip of his finger on the edge of his chin, grinning. "I know, shall I have them look at your fingertips?"

"My fingertips?" She instantly looked down, and that made him grin more.

"Yes, your fingertips. You probably still have dirt under your nails."

She began to turn red, and he knew he had her trapped. "See, killing someone isn't as easy as you think."

"Shhh! Just because you have it figured out doesn't mean I want the rest of the people to get it too! Keep this to yourself."

That's when he let his real smile show. "And that, Nadia, is what I want to give you, but I will need something in return."

"What is it?" she asked through gritted teeth.

"Convince Anabella to marry me. Agree to that, and then we can talk about keeping your itsy bitsy secret."

"You've been together for a year now. Deep down I hoped you were already secretly married so we wouldn't have to go through all that chaos of last year again."

"She doesn't want to set herself up for heartbreak. Whatever happened with Kain and his wife seems to have scared her."

Nadia sucked in a breath, and Carter watched her facial expressions change. "We don't like talking about Kain and Deanne. It was all so hard when things got bad."

"You and Carlisle seem to be doing just fine," he said in a soft and compassionate tone.

"We're different. I've always been different."

"How about this? I will help you trick all these people, we will have a blast doing it, and you at least try to work on your sister, soften her up. Because one way or another, I want her forever."

"Will you move to Cedar Rapids?"

Carter laughed loudly enough to make the others look at him with a questioning glare. He shrugged them off and returned his focus back onto Nadia. "No, but she can have her home in Cedar Rapids, and we can come visit frequently, or the family could come to Houston. We can make it work. Lots of couples live away from their families and make it."

He could tell Nadia was thinking about something, but he didn't want to pressure her. This was going to be his best option for finding an ally in the marriage department. "What do you say, Mrs. Ali? Will you help me become your brother?"

She looked up at him and gave him a wide, toothy smile. "You're already my brother, Carter, but yes, I will help you."

"Good. Now, tell me who the next victim is and how you want to execute it, and we can start from there."

Nadia looked around the room at the different partners and let her eyes rest on Charles. Carter smiled when he saw this and nodded. "Good pick, and the weapon of choice?" Nadia's eyes continued searching and finally rested on a candlestick that was holding one of the light sources for the evening's party.

Carter brought his hand to his chin and began to rub it, thinking about what he would do with the candlestick if it was him in this position. Then he grinned. "Since they want to do fingerprinting and what not, we will need to have almost everyone touch this candlestick. Let's place it around the room where people might have to touch it to move it, like on the table. Hand it to me, and then I'll go set it down in someone's way."

She nodded her head and reached over. She picked up the metal candle holder and placed it in Carter's hand. He turned around and sat it down on Carlisle's table section and then came back to Nadia, smiling. "Step one, alternative answer. Always need to remember to make sure it is plausible that someone else did the crime. If the weapon has several prints on it, then that is enough cause to say it wasn't you; it could have been anyone."

"Can't they tell whose prints were on there last?"

"People will most likely not touch the candlestick in the same place. When you picked it up you grabbed it on the bottom and I grabbed the top when I took it from you. Since I placed it on Carlisle's seat and he will most likely be sitting when he reaches for it, he will probably reach for the center of the object. When we go to move it again, you and I will remember to touch the same section we did before and then just hope the fourth and fifth people who reach for it touch it in separate places. But you see, at least three people's prints will clearly be on it, and that is enough to get a not guilty verdict."

He watched Nadia as he explained all this to her and realized that she wasn't exactly how he had pictured her. Yes, she was a nosey news reporter, but she was also more calculating. She had a clear look on her face when she was calculating risk or thinking about an outcome, and he liked that. It was good to him to see this, because it showed how intelligent she really was.

"Since we need to continue to set up distractions like this, I think I want murder number three to be committed with a knife."

Carter raised his eyebrow at her questioningly. "And I want to use Donna's dinner knife for it." It made him grin hearing her say that.

"Perfect. We will go get it before they take it away from the table." Carter started to move towards the table when Nadia's hand shot out and stopped his forward movement.

"Use a napkin. I only want her prints on this one."

He nodded his head and started walking towards Donna's spot on the table. He passed by the others, who were talking about the murder, and he caught Carlisle's eye. He wished there was some way to hint to his brother that he was in on it with Nadia, because he knew Carlisle had to know, but then again, it had been a long time since he'd played a prank on the big bad Mr. A. Maybe this time he could have a bit of fun of his own.

He knelt down and pretended to fix his shoe. No one paid attention to him as he stood up, palmed the napkin at Donna's seat, and then quickly picked up the knife and slipped it into his pocket. As he made his way back over to Nadia, he couldn't help grinning. She looked like she was having a lot of fun and had something on her mind to tell him.

"I got your knife," he said.

"And I have the perfect victim number three."

"Oh? And who is going to be the lucky person?"

"The man who least expects it." Her eyes looked around the room and rested on the one man who could scare paint off the wall.

"Carlisle Ali."

CHAPTER SIX

Anabella watched from across the room as her sister and boyfriend whispered secrets to one another. Carter kept moving around and doing different things. She didn't understand why he kept playing with objects, first the candlestick and then something with his shoe and the napkin. It wasn't even logical, but she decided it wasn't important for now and focused on what Mr. A was saying.

"Did you hear me, Ana?"

"Sorry, I was paying too much attention to Carter."

Carlisle shook his head in sympathy. "Love does that, takes all your attention."

"Yeah, it does, but something is going on over there with our dinner dates, and I can't seem to put my finger on it."

"Maybe they are conspiring against you?" he offered as a solution.

"Doubtful. You know it is hard to conspire against the Maverick women. We are thick as thieves and bonded through blood."

"Oh, I know all right, but that doesn't mean a man can't try."

She tilted her head to the side and gave him a look. "Can't try what?"

"Nothing. Come on; let's look at the body."

They walked over to where Casey's pretend lifeless body laid almost still. Everyone chose to ignore the fact his stomach moved up and down with each breath he took in and let out. It seemed like the group of people were being good sports, and that was going to help make this a fun day.

"Tell me what you see, Ana."

She looked the body over and didn't say anything for a few minutes. She knelt down and did her best to remember what she saw the television cops do on Law and Order when they were out trying to solve a murder. Then she remembered her favorite detective show, Psych, and how, many times, when Shawn and Gus were on a case, they would find some kind of footprint. That was when it hit her. She looked a few inches away from the body and saw a bit of dirt and a footprint, well, a partial footprint in the dirt.

Anabella moved closer to the dirt spot, careful not to touch anything that might affect the crime scene. She tilted her head to the side, did her own mental analysis of the spot, and smiled. The killer is a woman. She knew shoes. She loved shopping, and this shoe print definitely came from a woman. She didn't know the exact size, but it looked like if she put her shoe over it there would be a very close match. She stood up, grinning at Carlisle, and pointed towards the corner. They moved over in that direction.

"I have it narrowed down to two people!" she said with excitement.

"How did you do that so quickly?" he asked.

"I found a shoe print in the dirt by the body. It is a girl, probably a size seven and a half, so that leaves Donna and my sister."

"And you," he pointed out.

Anabella shook her head back and forth. "No, I know I'm not the killer, but you raise a good point. If I let this fact out, they might suspect me too." She thought about this for a moment and then gave a single nod. "It's Nadia. I'm sure of it."

"How can you be so sure?"

"Easily. She and Carter have been over there whispering, and he has been doing all these weird things, so Nadia must have told him her secret, and now he is going to cover up for her, help her."

"Don't you think you are stretching it a bit? Let's say that is Nadia's footprint. That could have gotten there when we all hovered around the body. You don't really have proof it wasn't there before that moment. We didn't secure the crime scene very well."

"Now you are protecting her. I'm right. It is Nadia, isn't it?"

Carlisle looked down at her and shook his head. "No, Ana, you are not right, or if you are, I don't know you're right. I'm just trying to help you see the holes in your case that will keep it from being an open and shut victory. Just don't shut off your eyes to another possibility."

"I hear you," she said and gave a slight wink. "You are protecting my sister, and I'll help protect her too."

For the next hour, they all moved around the room, trying to find more clues and sharing what they all had learned. In reality, it was Donna and Charles who did the most sharing, and what they shared didn't even make sense, like their makeshift fingerprinting system. They wanted to find a plastic baggie and some superglue. Someone had seen in a movie in which the characters put a plastic bag with superglue inside around a glass and fingerprints showed up. They wanted to test all of the glasses so they could attempt to identify the fingerprints on the potted plant.

Anabella supposed this was a good idea, but she didn't see how a bunch of people without any training could differentiate all of the lines. She assumed the two men with her would be able to, but if Nadia was the killer, she didn't think either of them were going to rat her out.

This posed a question for Anabella. Would she be the one to turn her sister in?

A ringing noise suddenly came from the speakers, and then a voice came over the microphone.

"Guests, please move to your seats so we can finish the dinner. We have a delectable dessert we want you to try."

Anabella thought this was odd, dinner while the fake dead body was sitting right next to them, but shrugged the weirdness off. It was all staged anyway. It wasn't like there was any real killings going on.

There was random small talk over the dessert course, and everyone seemed to be back into the mode of detective, trying to decide which of their companions were going to turn up dead next. Anabella couldn't stop looking at her sister. While she knew this was just a game, she somehow looked at Nadia in a new light. She had stepped off the good mild-mannered reporter stage and dove into the fake criminal element. Sometimes she wondered how much the marriage to Mr. A had changed Nadia.

"You're deep into thought there, my dear." The voice of Carter flowing slowly into her ear made her smile. Having him near her always made her smile, no matter what was going on.

"Just looking at my sister in a new light."

"Oh yeah, what light is that?" he said lowly.

"The light of a killer."

Carter chucked and shook his head back and forth. "You Maverick women, always jumping to conclusions."

"What, you don't think she could be the one? Carlisle didn't think so either."

"I have been around a long time and seen more than most people could imagine, so one thing I have learned ... never underestimate a woman. That being said, your sister does not seem the killer type."

"Maybe not in real life, but what about in staged murder mystery dinner?"

"You two always have the most intense imaginations." He leaned over and kissed her cheek, then began to eat his dessert. "So tell me why you think it's her. Give me your reasoning."

"First, I don't know if I can trust you now. You've been consorting with the enemy."

Carter bellowed out a laugh. It was deep and piercing. Everyone in the room turned their heads and looked over at them. If she was trying to keep attention away from herself, then this wasn't the way to go about it. "I know my sister's shoe size. That's all I am going to say to you, since you seem to think I am so funny." She crossed her arms and turned slightly away from him. She caught Nadia and Carlisle's stare as they both looked at her with a questioning gaze. She turned her head up in the air, away from Carter. She wasn't going to dignify anything with a response.

"Now, Anabella, come on. You know I'm always on your side. Why would I conspire with your sister to go against you?"

She turned her head slightly so she could see him out of her peripheral. "Because."

"That's it? Because?"

She gave a swift nod.

"Darling, you are going to need more than that to convince me of anything. So you know her shoe size. I know Carlisle's too. That doesn't mean he's a killer."

"Look," she said in a huff. She turned her body around to face him and kept her voice low but sharp. "I know what I saw. It is Nadia, and I am going to win this game. Are you with me or against me?"

She watched his eyes. Most people didn't know when he was lying because he covered it up so well, but she could tell when he was keeping something from her. It was in his eyes. The left one twitched a little above his eyelid, right below the eyebrow, every time he wanted to say something but kept it inside. She saw the same spot twitch, and she knew she was right. He was in on it, and he was keeping it from her.

"You're very smart, Ana. You know I love that about you, right?"

"Don't change the subject, Carter." She smiled at him. "But I do love hearing you say that. Both things, actually, I love hearing."

"I know you do. Do you want to get out of here and go enjoy a dinner alone, just the two of us?" He reached his arm out and pulled her slightly to him, close enough that he could kiss her if he leaned his head in just slightly.

Anabella pushed away from him and said, "You're distracting me again. I am finishing out this night."

Carter sighed, looked back to his plate, and finished eating his dessert. She took a glance over at her sister, who she noticed was eyeing her intently. She flashed a smile to Nadia, shrugged her shoulders, and then tilted her head in the direction of Carter, as if to say she didn't know what was up with him. She only hoped she was putting Nadia off the trail.

Anabella stopped a moment from thinking her next thought to focus on that last thing. She knew it was Nadia. She knew Carter knew it was Nadia. Did Nadia know Carter knew it was Nadia? And would Nadia find out that Anabella knew it was Nadia? Of course she would, because Anabella had foolishly told Carlisle it was Nadia.

She shook her head back and forth a few times to try and clear her thoughts. It felt like a ping pong match going on inside of her head with all of the back and forth things she was thinking.

"If you all will excuse me, I need to find the ladies' room," she said to the table as she pushed her chair out and stood up. "Does anyone know where it is?"

"Ms. Maverick, the restroom is located beside the kitchen door," the voice over the speakers said.

She looked up and around the ceiling then called out, "Thank you!" She smiled to Carter and then over to her sister before walking towards the secluded room where she could take a minute and think.

"Nadia, I think Anabella is onto you," Carlisle whispered while eating a bite of dessert.

"What makes you say that?"

"Because she told me she knew it was you."

"How could she know it is me? She hasn't seen or been around me since it happened, and it isn't like we told her!" Nadia said, feeling a little flustered that her sister would have it figured out so easily.

"She found a shoe print that she swears is your size and said that she would know your shoe print anywhere."

"My shoe print!" She couldn't help feeling irritated that something so easy as a shoe print could tip off her sister. Since when did she know her shoes that well? "We will have to throw her off then."

"I don't know how you are going to manage that."

"Well Carter knows it is me too. Apparently, I am not as sneaky as I thought I was."

"Reporters never are, love."

"I used to be before I got saddled with the criminal element."

"I do believe you were around the criminal element long before I came into your life, my pet."

"Well I didn't associate with them on a daily basis. They were just sources I used for stories. You're different. You're making me soft!"

Carlisle laughed out loud, reached his arm around his wife's shoulders, leaned into her, and kissed the top of her head. "If I have made you soft, my pet, I am so sorry. I shall make it up to you, I promise."

"In the meantime we have to do something while she is in the bathroom to throw her off of me. Carter says he will keep my secret if I help get Ana to marry him."

"He is probably enjoying teaming up with you for something. It will naturally put Ana on edge, and men like Carter and I like throwing our women off."

"Oh you do, huh? And how often do you throw me off, Mr. A?"

"I plead the fifth."

"We're not in America; that doesn't work here."

"Oh yeah it does." He patted her on the head with his palm.

She swatted his hand away from the top of her head and laughed with a delight in her voice that she only had when he was teasing her. Kain used to tease her that she sounded like a little schoolgirl when Carlisle was around, but she didn't mind. After two years of him teasing her, she wouldn't have anyone else in the picture.

"I'm going to have to do the next killing now while she is in the bathroom so she doesn't see me do it."

"Won't that be obvious if she is onto you and you magically do it while she's away?"

"What other choice do I have?" Nadia asked Carlisle.

He sighed and then smiled. "All right, good point. So who is victim number two, and what are you using?"

"I can't tell you all my secrets. It isn't fair to everyone else."

"You're holding out on me? My pet, what has Carter done to you? I leave you with him for five minutes, and you are already holding out details of our plans."

"Our plans? Last I checked, this was my show." She grinned up at him and then looked at the candlestick that now was in Jason's hand. He had picked it up when Carlisle placed it in front of Jason's seat when he came back to the table.

"Ahh, I was wondering why that was by my seat."

"Yeah, that was Carter's idea. Help throw people off the scent if they figure out how to do fingerprinting techniques while in the middle of dinner."

"Good idea. Well, little lady, you'd better get to it."

With a large smile, Nadia looked around and clicked the lights off.

When Anabella walked into the bathroom, she saw the walls were decorated in a red velvet wall covering. There were detailed designs sewn into the different layers, giving the shapes of lions and tigers throughout the whole bathroom. There was a golden tint that shimmered off of the light against the wall. Anabella had never seen anything so detailed and beautiful.

She let her fingertips run over the designs along the wall and felt mesmerized by the delicacy of each stitch. She wondered how long they had been on the wall. From what she'd read, this hotel and resort hadn't had major renovations done since the early 1900's except for the light system and air-conditioning. She doubted that the bathrooms fell under those categories. How had people managed to make something so beautiful before machine technology had assisted in the stitching?

Upon her return to the front lobby after tonight's dinner, she was going to make it a point to ask about the detailing on the walls. Anabella hadn't paid enough attention to the rooms' decor to remember if they also looked like this. She made a mental note to check that out too once tonight's festivities were finished.

There were two stalls inside the bathroom. She pushed the first door open and turned around to lock it securely. She had just sat on the white porcelain seat when she felt a sudden shock as the lights went out and then a few seconds later turned back on.

She had missed the next murder.

Putting herself together quickly, she rushed out of the bathroom and returned to the dinner party to see that Charles was now lying on the floor. There was a semi-circle of people gathered around him, and the candlestick that Carter had previously held was now lying alongside the pretend lifeless body.

Anabella was convinced now more than anything that not only was Nadia the killer but Carter was in on this as well.

"Ana," Nadia called out and then raised her hand and waved her over to them. She didn't know what she should do, pretend she knew nothing, or call out Nadia on the killings. After taking a deep breath, she walked towards her sister and the guys and put on a smile to make it through this next session.

CHAPTER SEVEN

"I need to speak with you," Anabella whispered into Nadia's ear. She looked up at her sister and then over at Carlisle. Everything they had just spoken about flashed through her mind, and she didn't want to stop her fun just yet. She was going to figure out a way to deflect the situation. "What's up, sis?"

"What did I miss?" Anabella asked softly.

"Just as you were going to the bathroom, Jason got up and walked over to Charles. They were talking about something in secret when the lights went out, and then Charles was on the ground."

"You think Jason did it?" Anabella asked.

Nadia knew that her sister was trying to goad her into answering in a way that would get her caught in a lie, so simply shrugged her shoulders and decided to play dumb. "I'm not sure. Anything is possible, I guess." Then she got an idea; she would talk to Anabella about what Carter had mentioned to her. "Hey, so not to change the subject but..." She paused trying to think how to phrase the next sentence. She knew her sister was anti-marriage and believed the only way she could help Carter achieve what he wanted was to bring it up to her first. "I hear Carter really wants to make things official."

Anabella's surprise was clearly expressed on her face. Nadia didn't think it was that shocking, but clearly her sister had a different idea.

"What makes you say that?" she asked, sounding shocked.

A grin came over Nadia's face, and she said, "Because he told me so. Did you not think he was thinking about it? Come on, you two are practically adjoined at the hip."

Part of her wanted to jump up and down and get her sister all excited about the idea of marriage, but she knew how Anabella thought about the lifelong commitment after the disaster of Kain's situation.

"I don't know..." Anabella's voice was very quiet and almost sounded shaky.

"What don't you know?"

"I don't know if I can do the whole, 'until death do you part' bit. I mean, look at Kain."

"You have to stop using our brother like that. He doesn't like it, and neither do I."

"But," Anabella paused and then took a deep breath. "I know. I'm just scared."

"Well, aren't we all scared? I mean, hell, look at me. I took a huge leap of faith with Carlisle, and see how happy I am! Can't you focus on that?"

"Kain was happy too, at first."

Nadia shook her head back and forth and tried to hold her tongue. This wasn't the right venue for a real relationship debate, but she had made a promise to try and help Carter. "It isn't that cut and dry, Ana."

She watched her sister shrug her shoulders and then continued. "You love him, don't you?"

Anabella nodded a few times and then looked at her sister. "I do, a lot."

"And you spend, like, every weekend with him, right? And sometimes even the whole week if he is in Cedar Rapids."

"Yeah, but—"

"No, hear me out. If you are already doing all of this, what are you so scared of?"

"It changing."

Nadia smiled at that. "Of course it will change. It will get better. The intimacy gets more intense, and everything will just grow in greatness. Trust me, I never thought Carlisle and I would be this close, but we are, and it is such a great feeling. I want you to have this happiness too."

Anabella looked at Nadia sharply and then asked, "Hey what brought this on all of a sudden?"

This caused Nadia to pause for a second, but she had a retort ready. "Well, this is the first time we are sort of alone to talk since Carter told me he wanted to marry you, so I jumped on the chance."

"When did he tell you this?"

"Earlier, after Charles was killed and we were off in the corner talking. All he could talk about was you and what he hoped you would agree too."

"Is that why he brought me here? To Africa?"

"That, girlie, I have no idea about. I simply know what he told me. He asked me to help. I told him I would love to push you in the right direction. You can be a stubborn woman, and occasionally you need a swift kick in the rear."

"So glad to see that you are all about the compassion there, sister."

"Always, Ana, always."

It was then that Carter and Carlisle walked up to them and looked down at each woman. Nadia knew her face held a touch of deviousness on it and saw Carlisle's natural reaction appear on his face.

"Carter, we are in trouble. I know that look on Nadia's face."

Nadia gasped and fanned herself in shock. "What look?"

"Yes, my brother, I've gotten to know that look too over the last year. I feel sorry for you, my man."

Anabella laughed and nodded in agreement with Carter. "I too feel sorry for you, Carlisle. You really had no idea what you were getting into two years ago."

"Hello, I'm right here, people. I can hear all of you talking about me." Nadia waved her hands up and down for theatrical effect.

Carlisle leaned over and kissed the top of her head. "My pet, we know you are there, but that doesn't change anything. And you are right, Ana. I had no idea what I was getting into two years ago, but I am sure as hell glad I did. It's been a wild and fun ride."

"Well, glad someone is happy to have me around." Nadia crossed he arms over her chest and pouted. She could pretend to act like the sad female that women usually got accused of being if it suited the situation.

"Don't pout, my pet. It isn't becoming."

"I'll show you becoming. See what happens next time you talk about me as if I'm not even present."

"Simmer down, kids. We've got a murder to solve," Carter stated. Everyone in the room had turned their eyes on the four of them when Nadia's voice went up a few octaves as she bantered with Carlisle.

"Murder!" Anabella accidentally yelled out a little louder than needed. Nadia saw the other people in the room turn and look at their little huddle and instantly felt self-conscious.

Nadia had almost forgotten there was a room full of other people around her. When she started to take note of the room, she saw that the others had formed their own little cluster and were probably discussing the fake dead body.

How many people would become victims before they discovered it was her, she wondered.

"That's right," Anabella said in a more appropriate tone. She looked at her sister and pointed, then moved her finger to Carlisle and then Carter. In a lower voice, she said, "You are all in on it. I know it. Now, someone better start explaining, or I am going to out all three of you as killers."

"Ana, I told you I'm not," Nadia claimed.

"Shh, love, don't let the game get to you." Carter rubbed her shoulder.

"Be real, Ana. Do I look like a killer?"

"No, but this isn't real. Anyway, I know I'm right, so either let me in on it, or I'm gonna out you."

"Hey, you four, you going to help us solve the murder?" Donna yelled from across the room.

They all turned their heads and looked in the direction of the woman speaking. Nadia noticed that the other people were also paying attention to them. "Let's look at the body and see if we can figure anything out."

Nadia, Carlisle, Carter, and Anabella all walked over to Charles's body. Anabella knelt down and looked over the candlestick, analyzing the position it had fallen in. The other individuals were all joining her now as she looked over each section of Charles carefully. Suddenly, the speakers turned on and the voice came back over the intercom.

"Ladies and gentleman, this is the first round elimination. It is now time to guess who the murderer is. Please note that, if you guess wrong, you will be eliminated from the game."

Everyone looked to the front doors that were now opening and watched as the host walked in.

"Please gather round, everyone. It is time for the first round."

The people were silent as everyone waited for him to call on someone to give their first guess. Nadia felt the intensity of the situation pressing on her. Even though she knew the truth, what if she was asked to guess? She would automatically be eliminated. Then who would carry it on?

"The first contestant will be Oliver. Please come forward and give your best guess."

Relief flooded Nadia as she realized she wasn't going to be called. Then she realized she could be called out. Her mind started to wander; the reporter in her kicked in. Was this how it felt like for criminals who were waiting with baited breath to see if the police would catch them after a crime? She realized that the two experiences weren't close to being the same, since this was a stimulation, but she had to assume there were some realistic feelings going through her that the criminal element experienced too.

"Please provide us with your educated guess," the host said.

Oliver looked around the room and then focused his eyes on the Maverick group. He raised his hand and pointed in the Mavericks' direction. "You four, there is something about you."

They all held their breaths, waiting on the next comment. "I say that you, mister 'I'm a detective,' Carlisle. You are the killer."

The four of them let out a simultaneous breath and then smiled. Carlisle proudly spoke up. "I'm sorry, but I am not your killer."

Oliver's facial expression was one of genuine shock. He really was expecting Carlisle to be the killer. There was some ironic humor in that.

"Sorry, Oliver, you are removed from the game. You may finish watching from the side of the room."

The group of ten had now dwindled down to seven, four of whom knew who the killer was. This could get very interesting.

Carter had watched the last hour go by, and a lot had seemed to take place, when in reality, nothing had really changed. His sole focus had been on winning Anabella's love. He had purchased the ring before the trip. It was a yellow gem, because her favorite color was yellow. He kept it in his pocket at all times, waiting for the perfect moment. He wasn't sure why tonight felt like it was going to be the best moment of the trip. They still had three days left on their journey before they were supposed to head back home.

Anabella had looked so adorable accusing Nadia of being the fake killer. Truth be told, it was a turn on knowing that the woman he felt was his partner was able to pick out those little details at the scene of the crime to pinpoint the killer in such a short period without the use of any technology.

"Hey, you going to go back and join Nadia, or are you going to stay with me?" Anabella asked him as she turned around and started to walk back to her chair. He quickly followed close behind her. The movement of her hips was hypnotic to him and captivated his attention like flies to honey. When they sat down at the table, he grabbed her hand gently, brought it to his lips, and placed a soft kiss on it.

"I think we need to talk," Anabella said.

No man liked his woman starting a conversation with that. It was the start of a terrible conversation usually. "Yes, Ana?"

"Nadia said something to me earlier, and I wanted to talk to you about it."

She had lived up to her end of the bargain, it seemed. It was good to know Nadia had kept her word. Not that there was ever a doubt that she would. "What did she tell you?"

"She said that you were ready to get married."

"I see, and if that's true?"

"If it is true, then I—" Her voice was cut off when the lights went out again, and this time they didn't come back on.

The floor started to shake, and they could hear the building begin making noises. She reached out for him and felt him instantly grab onto her. "Get under the table!" he called out.

Once they were under the table, she realized Nadia and Carlisle weren't there. "Nadia!" she yelled.

"Ana!"

"Where are you?"

"We are coming to you," Carlisle yelled.

Carter and Anabella waited under the table as the floor shook yet again. He knew none of them had been involved in an earthquake before, and certainly none thought they would be in one while on a vacation. He and Carlisle had survival training, and that had covered this type of emergency. They just tried to avoid putting themselves in this position unless absolutely necessary.

"There is a fault line here?" Anabella asked as Nadia and Carlisle slid under the table.

"Yes, the Central African Shear Zone, but I had no idea it was going to activate while we were on vacation," Carlisle replied.

"Great, just what we needed." Carter looked around to see if he could see any change in the room at all. There was emergency light starting to turn on, and he could see that the other dinner guests were all crowded around one another in the middle of the floor. He had done a lot of night work when he was in the militia in South Africa. His mind and eyes were quick to adjust back to their old training, and survival mode kicked into gear. He thrived in situations like this, even if he hated the fact the ones he loved were here and not safely back home in the States.

In his opinion, this quake felt very close to a seven on the scale. He was sure there would be some more tremors later and little aftershocks. Honestly, he was surprised that the room itself hadn't suffered more damage than it had given how much stuff the room had in it.

Everything had happened so quickly. One minute they were teasing each other and laughing and the next minute, the ground had started to move. He wasn't sure how the rest of them felt, but to him it felt like he had suddenly been dropped into a theme park, trying to cross uneven ground that was constantly shaking.

His stomach felt shaken up, either from the nervousness of the situation or the up and down motion. He wasn't sure what did it, but a memory of a deep sea diving expedition flew into the forefront of his mind the moment he started walking on moving ground.

Now, he needed to focus on was Anabella and her family, his family.

"Carter?" Carlisle whispered.

He turned his head over his shoulder to look at his friend and saw he was pointing to something. He followed Carlisle's finger to the top corner of the room near one of the emergency lights and saw the crack in the ceiling that Carlisle had been pointing to.

"Girls," he said, "I think shit just got real."

Everyone was now looking at the corner of the wall that was cracking more and more with each passing minute. The room's tension was so solid that it couldn't have been cut with a knife.

"Carter, what do we do?" Anabella's voice was a whispered, but Carter could detect her panic. Carter didn't know what kind of training Anabella had received in her military career, but he as fairly sure that it hadn't consisted of this. Something told him that the room's only chance for survival if the building came down on them was him and Carlisle.

He looked to his brother-in-arms and said, "We need to get everyone to evacuate the room."

Carlisle nodded his head in agreement, and together they began to look around the room. The girls were between the two of them, and the sturdy table shielded them from any falling debris, but that would only work for so long. Soon the roof would come down, and nothing would be able to protect them from that.

"We need to open the door and see how the hallway looks." Carlisle moved out from under the table and quickly made it to the door. Everyone watched him tap the handle a couple times. Carter assumed he was checking to make sure there wasn't a fire out in the hallway. When the door opened everyone could see what was in front of him.

Debris.

Part of the building had already collapsed, and as of right now, they were trapped inside this room. Carter looked back up to the corner of the ceiling. The crack was still growing. It wasn't at a rapid speed, but it was noticeable.

"We all need a plan," Carlisle said to the room. "Everyone, please, let's gather around." He looked through the people standing and took a count of everyone who was around. Oliver had joined his brother,

Charles. Casey, Donna, Jason, and Steve were all in a small huddle off to his left, across the room. Anabella, Nadia, and Carter were gathered under the table in self-preservation mode.

Anabella, Nadia, and Carter all came out from under the table and met Carlisle in the middle of the room. They watched as the rest of the people joined them. Everyone seemed to be okay. Well, that was, everyone who had been involved in playing the dinner murder game.

"Has anyone ever been in an earthquake before?" Jason asked the group.

Only one person spoke up. "I have, back in California, but it was only a 3.7, and we had no damage." Oliver looked like he was still in shock from the quake. Carter knew he wasn't going to be of any use.

The ground started to shake again, and Anabella reached out and grabbed his arm. He pulled her close and balanced their weight together. Everyone looked up to the crack in the ceiling at the same time. "Those aftershocks, how long can they last?" He tossed the question out to the general room. Carlisle was the one who answered.

"Days, and sometimes years. There is no telling how many there will be. We just have to hope it was only one."

"How are we going to get out of here? What about another exit?" Donna's voice was full of panic. Typically people don't have to experience these types of situations while on vacation, and it required a strong sense of calm and leadership to get people out of these positions safely. Lucky for all of these people, Mr. A and Mr. J were up for the job.

"Follow me. Let's check the kitchen route." Carlisle led the group of people slowly across the floor. Carter hung back a little bit to make sure he brought up the tail end of the group, Anabella's hand securely inside his. Everyone stopped when Carlisle couldn't push open the kitchen door.

"Nadia, give me your phone."

"You think we have reception?" she asked, pulling it out of her pocket.

"No, I think you have a flashlight." He turned on the white beam of light and placed it up to the window of the kitchen door. Everyone saw the same thing as the light shone in the window.

There was a large piece of furniture or an appliance blocking the door.

No one was getting in or out through this exit either. Everyone moved back into the middle of the room, and Nadia was the first to sit down. Carter watched as Anabella sat beside her and put her arm around her younger sister's shoulders. One by one, everyone joined them, until Carter and Carlisle were the last two people standing.

CHAPTER EIGHT

Nadia's heart was racing. She was going to give serious though to seeing a spiritual advisor when she got back home. She was pretty sure that there wasn't one anywhere in Cedar Rapids, but she was sure there were some in Houston. She would make a point of seeing one every time that she was down there to visit with Anabella. Her karma had to be off for disasters to keep happening to her like this no matter where she was.

The logical part of her knew that this had nothing to do with her, it was just nature, but she still felt like she might be somewhat cursed.

Then a thought hit her. She was pregnant. She hasn't told Carlisle! What would she do if she lost the baby? She could feel her heart start to race more and more. She needed to calm it down, refocus on the situation and not the growing body inside her stomach. Nadia would simply have to do everything in her power to protect that little child, even if he or she was only a few weeks old.

She looked over at her sister, who was helping to calm Donna down. She assumed her sister was used to this, being the calm one in the middle of a disaster. As close as the two of them were, Anabella still kept silent about her stint in the military. Kain had always told her that Anabella's past life was just that, in the past, but watching her stay cool and calm now gave Nadia a different look at her sister.

"Nadia, come here please," she heard Mr. A's voice say. That helped to pull her mind off of the pregnancy. Why had he used that tone and not the normal loving tone of Carlisle's? This wasn't the man she'd married, but the calculated man she had attempted to stalk and fallen in love with. Moving quickly, she got up and went over to his side.

"Yes?"

"Go put all of the water from the table into one container. We don't know how long we are going to be stuck, and we need to conserve the water to keep us all hydrated. Then, once that's done, get together the leftover food that hasn't been touched. We will need everything we can in the event we can't be rescued right away."

She nodded once and then rushed over to the table and began doing her assigned tasks. At least this time she was with Carlisle during the crisis. The other times she'd found herself in trouble, she had always been alone. Not that having the people she loved trapped with her made her any calmer about the situation, but she did find comfort knowing that she wouldn't have to carry this all on her shoulders alone.

"Do you need some help?" She looked around and saw Casey walking toward her. She gave a simple nod, and silently they worked together to clear the table of the food and water that could be salvaged.

"Sorry I killed you earlier," she said in a whisper. His eyebrows shot up in a questioning stare as he looked back at her. "What, you don't think I'm capable?"

"You're a tiny woman. I would hate to think that you would be able to take me out in a real battle."

She laughed a real laugh. It was nice to know that some people around here thought she looked like a harmless, carefree lady. "While I think most women would be hurt if a man had such little faith in them, I am quite pleased! Thank you for thinking I looked mild-mannered and innocent."

"Ha, I never said that! I just said that I didn't think you could take me in a fight."

Nadia watched Carlisle come walking up behind Casey and smiled. "Well, either way, it is a complement that you think I look defenseless.

We have been working hard on bringing out my innocent appearance. Right, darling?"

Carlisle patted Casey on the shoulder as he came alongside the man. "That's right. We work hard to keep this one innocent."

"All your talk makes me wonder what it is you guys do for a living." Casey had a playful tone, but Nadia knew he was serious. People always questioned Carlisle. It was something they were very used to.

"Nadia, are you almost done? Carter and I want to talk with you and Anabella."

"Yes, I am." She finished putting her things together quickly in a secure container then walked over to her family. Anabella and Nadia listened as Carter began speaking.

"We are going to build a safe zone over here, in this corner, near the exit. This way, when the rescue party comes, they have a better chance of finding us."

"Because we are near the exit?" Nadia asked.

"Yes, but also because the outer frames of buildings tend to be the strongest, so there is less of a chance the walls at the corner will fall compared to other ones, giving us a better chance and more protection."

"What are we going to use for cover?" Anabella asked while looking around the room.

"We were thinking about the table, maybe propping it up against the wall on a tilt so any debris can slide away from us."

"Will we all be able to fit there?" Nadia looked around the room at the others who were not standing and watching them.

"I'm not sure, but it will work for us, and we are all I care about right now," Carter replied in a cold toned voice.

"You all know we can hear you, right?" Charles had moved forward. His arms were crossed over his chest, and his face was giving off a seriously pissed off look.

"Did you hear something you didn't like?" Carlisle moved to stand in front of their group in a protective stance.

"Well, the rest of us have been talking, and we don't like how you two seem to think you are in charge."

"Oh, is that so? Well, Bub, do you want to be in charge?"

Donna spoke up. "I don't think anyone—" She was abruptly cut off when Charles turned his head quickly and gave her a very evil look.

"Did anyone ask for your opinion, woman? No, now let the men talk."

Nadia knew what was about to happen. Carlisle and Carter may not have relinquished control of the situation based on one foolish man, but they were definitely not going to allow a woman to be disrespected like that, especially in front of people.

"Buddy, I think you owe Donna an apology," Carter said, stepping beside Carlisle.

"I'm not going to apologize to some dumb broad. Now, you two, stop hogging all of the time and furniture. You four are going to do what we say."

"Charles, if I were you—" Nadia tried to speak, but Carlisle raised his hand in the air, and she knew that she needed to be silent.

"At least your bitch stays on her leash."

And that was the straw that broke the camel's back, so to speak. Carlisle was on Charles within a blink of an eye. No one saw the punch coming. Carlisle moved so fast that all anyone heard was the cracking of Charles's jaw.

Carlisle hadn't knocked him out, so when he stepped back, away from Charles, Nadia was able to see the look in his eye as he rubbed his jaw where Carlisle had just punched him. She knew it was coming. She called out, "Carlisle watch out!"

By that time, Charles had already begun to swing. Carlisle was hit on the side of his shoulder as he backed away. From that point, Nadia watched Carlisle push off the balls of his feet and jump into the air to land on Charles. The punches began to fly both ways. The other people in the room began to talk; some were yelling. Nadia wasn't sure what they were saying. All she cared about was Carlisle.

She raced over to the two men, but Carter caught her by her waist to keep her from getting in the middle of the fight.

"Carlisle, stop!" she yelled. He didn't reply. He didn't even act as if he heard her.

"Mr. A! Help! Mr. A! Stop!" she tried screaming.

Tears were running down her face, and she felt Anabella and someone else holding her shoulders back. Why was no one stopping them? She didn't understand.

She wiggled her way loose of the two people holding her, and she ran towards the two men. She jumped onto them and pushed them apart. When she was standing between them, she looked from Carlisle to Charles. When Charles began to approach her in an aggressive stride, the same form she had just seen him attack her husband in, she lifted her leg out and extended it with as much force as she could.

The target and receiving end of her kick was his genitals. He was down for the count, and the room silenced. She looked over at Carlisle and moved her eyes over his body to ensure he was okay. Then she turned her head towards Carter, who quickly came over and removed Carlisle from the scene of the fight.

"You bitch, you kicked me!" Charles's voice was full of agony, and she didn't care.

"You goaded my husband. You gave me no choice."

"He hit first."

"After you insulted me. Now shut up and let us figure out a way to save all our asses, or maybe they should just let you die off."

Nadia walked away and into Anabella's arms. Her heart was racing, and her mind was spinning. This couldn't be good for her child, she thought. She had to calm down.

Had all that really just happened? What had come over Carlisle to behave so foolishly? Deep down, she knew. The man had insulted her, and Carlisle couldn't tolerate that. It was a slap against everything he believed in when it involved someone he loved.

"Nadia, help me gather the food, that way we can make sure Charles doesn't get his hands on it." Nadia quickly followed her sister, and moments later, Donna came up behind them. The three women silently put everything in what they thought was a safe place while Carter and Carlisle began to move the heavy dining room table.

Eventually, the other men except for Charles helped Carter and Carlisle push the table over to the corner that they all deemed the sturdiest. Since no one there was an engineer, they were just guessing, but hopefully the educated guess would pan out as the correct one. They picked a corner near the front door and furthest away from the cracked ceiling. Hopefully they wouldn't need all the preparation, but it was better safe than sorry, the way they all saw it.

"Are you okay?" Nadia eventually asked Carlisle. He hadn't said much to her as they moved around. He was most likely embarrassed about how he had behaved and now didn't want to admit how much control he had lost all because of her.

"I'm fine. Let's just focus on working."

"I'd like to talk to you, if you can spare a second, Carlisle."

"Later."

"Now."

"Nadia, I said later. Please don't argue on this one."

She didn't like how his tone had been with her. She pushed him away from everyone and into a more private area. She had to tell him now about the baby. She couldn't keep it in when they were in a life and death situation "What if there isn't any later?"

"I'll never let anything happen to you, my pet."

"Even the great Mr. A can't control natural disasters. Just look at what has already happened." She sighed and then reached for his hand, brought it to her lips, and kissed it. "I love you."

"I love you too."

"Can you go make peace with Charles so we can all work safely? I don't think he will do anything else, but you can never be too sure."

"Did you hurt yourself?" he asked in a low tone.

"Hurt myself? When? Kicking him? God no!"

"Okay, good, because I wouldn't be okay with myself if you had gotten hurt."

"I know you probably hate what I did."

He nodded his head a few times.

"But someone had to stop you!"

"I know. That doesn't mean I like that you had to do it."

"Well, I get why you were set off. I would have been too if I were in your shoes."

"I'm glad you understand, I'm sorry."

"I love you, Carlisle. You don't have anything to apologize for."

"Not used to this, losing control of stuff. Usually, you are the one to go off the deep end."

"Ha. Ha," she said in a dry, fake laugh.

Carlisle leaned over and kissed her. He let his arms wrap around her body and held her close to him. Their warmth reassured her, something she really needed right now.

"There is something else–" she started to say before she was cut off.

"You two coming back?" Carter yelled out after them.

"Yeah, brother, just a sec."

"Don't take all day," Carter retorted.

"I'll go make up with Charles," Carlisle whispered to her.

He kissed her again and then left. He had vanished before she'd had the chance to tell him.

After two hours of organizing and reconstructing different parts of the room, the safety corner was now as secured as it could be. There was enough room for each person to sit somewhat comfortably and places to store the food and water that everyone had equal access too. There was no telling how long the walls would hold, and Anabella was nervous that people would get too anxious and get cabin fever waiting for the rescue.

"Do you hear that?" asked Oliver.

Everyone in the room silenced themselves, and they all sat patiently, waiting to hear whatever noise had made Oliver call out.

"I hear it!" Jason smiled and said, "It's our rescue!"

"Help, help! We're in here!" Donna yelled out. Steve raced to the front door and began banging on it. The noise echoed in the room, and Anabella looked up instantly at the crack.

"Stop," she said. The word didn't have a lot of volume to it; only Nadia had heard her. Anabella motioned for Nadia to look up and see the crack growing bigger. That noise wasn't someone coming to rescue them. It was the building beginning to fall more.

"STOP!" Anabella screamed at the top of her lungs. Everyone turned around and looked at her. She pointed to the ceiling and then looked to the corner safety area. "We gotta get protected now."

They all began to run. It wasn't very far to make it from across the room, but when everyone was making a mad dash in the same direction, trying to go into the same small entrance, there was a jam. Anabella and Nadia made it inside the secured section first, followed closely by Steve, Jason, and Donna. Then came Carter and Carlisle. Casey and Oliver straggled in, and then last came Charles. He knelt down at the entry of the secured section and looked around.

"Doesn't look like there is enough room for me too," he said.

"There is if you behave yourself," Nadia retorted.

"I think I'll take my chances with the building and lead myself away from this snake pit."

"Charles, wait," Oliver protested. Anabella noticed that Oliver moved to go after Charles but stopped when Charles lifted up a hand, palm outward, in Oliver's direction.

Charles replied with a simple statement, "Goodbye."

Carter put the cloth they had rigged as a door in his hand. "Fine with us. Be safe." And he locked Charles out of the safety zone.

The nine of them all looked at one another as the building began shaking again. They didn't know if it was another aftershock or if it was the building beginning to crumble on its own. Either way, the walls were moving, and they could hear the debris falling on top of the table and other items they had used to secure this spot.

The dust was kept to a minimum inside the cubby hole thanks to the idea Donna had had about draping the cloth around the inside so people wouldn't have to worry about breathing. "This was a good idea, Donna."

"Thank you, Carter." Donna blushed at the complement.

"Carlisle, this is why women will always be the superior sex, they think of the convenience factor stuff."

Almost everyone laughed a little. Anabella noticed that Oliver had kept his head hanging down since Charles had chosen not to join them.

It helped lighten the mood, listening to the conversation about convenience items and women. They were getting through this trauma. Then they heard the scream. It was Charles. They all knew it was him. Not only had it sounded like a death scream, it sounded like a man who was terrified.

Anabella didn't want to see what had happened to him. The room was still shaking, and things were still not going as well as anyone had hoped. Life was changing all around them now.

"Charles!" Oliver yelled. "I need to go check on him!" Everyone knew he was scared for his brother. They were all scared for Charles.

"If you go out there, you risk dying too." Jason said what everyone was thinking.

"He's my brother. I have to."

"Let Oliver go," Carlisle commanded.

Carter removed the makeshift door cloth, and Oliver peeked his head outside into the room. "Oh my god," he said before moving his whole body out of the safety of the group and into the rubble.

"Godspeed," someone said.

Anabella looked around and questioned, "Godspeed ?" to no one in particular.

Everyone sat there silently, waiting to hear if anything came of the search for Charles. Anabella hoped that Oliver would be okay. She hadn't seen anything that indicated he was as big of an ass as his brother, so she hoped he wouldn't suffer any bad fate.

"Help! Someone come help me!" Oliver finally yelled.

No one moved. They all stayed still inside the privacy of their protection.

"Please, someone help. He needs help!"

"That was the risk he took," Jason yelled.

Everyone was looking back and forth at each other. Anabella saw Nadia looking from Carter to Carlisle, and her heart sped up. "No, you two aren't going. I'm putting my foot down this time."

"Ana..." Carter said.

"Look, you want to marry me, and you," she pointed to Carlisle, "married my sister. That means we are your priorities. I won't lose either of you. No way."

"I agree with Ana," Nadia said. "You two are always helping people back home. This once, you are going to put us first."

The four of them looked around at the others, who were staring back at them. "Sorry," Anabella said. "Our family has been through a lot, and I just can't risk losing them. No one can force someone to go out there, so we won't force any of you to go either."

"If it was my child out there, I'd want someone to help," Donna said.

"If it was a child, none of this would be an issue, as we wouldn't have let a child go off on their own, but those two made their decisions," Carlisle stated boldly.

"Help, someone, please! I'll give anything," Oliver was still calling out.

Yet no one moved.

CHAPTER NINE

"Don't you think he has been out there a long time without saying anything?" Donna asked.

"It's his own fault. I thought we all agreed on that," Steve said.

"But that doesn't mean I don't care. I just don't want to risk rocking the boat or anything."

Nadia was listening to these two people talk. They thought everyone was asleep, but she could still hear their whispered voices. She too felt bad for not doing anything to go out there and help them, but what would she have done? She didn't have the kind of training that Mr. A and Mr. J had, or even the kind that Anabella had, and more importantly, why risk herself or the baby for someone who didn't even care about women?

Exactly, there wasn't any point, so she simply tuned out Donna and Steve and hoped that she would find a way to drift off to sleep so she could get some rest.

It felt like only a few moments had passed since she'd had the last thought, but she wasn't sure. When Carlisle woke her up, he said it was time to go take inventory on what had happened, that the ground and walls had stopped moving for a while now, and it was finally safe to go see what had happened to the other two dinner guests.

Everyone gave their opinion on who should go outside and take a look around. None of the women voted to go. They all decided they were best staying in the dust free zone. Jason and Casey both stayed with them, under the guise that, if something happened, there would need to be men around to help the women. That left Steve, Carter and Carlisle to go out and fetch the brothers back.

Carter pulled down the makeshift door once again, and the three men left the safe zone in single file. Not a word was heard from Carter or Carlisle as they exited, but Steve that was a different story. Everyone heard him gasp in shock when he saw the destruction.

"Maybe we should have gone outside with them, so we could see how bad it is," Anabella said.

"Join them if you want, but I have no desire to risk getting hurt. You know how lucky I am about those trip hazards." Nadia smiled at her sister.

"True, I remember my ankle sprain last year. I'll just stay tight." Anabella laughed lightly, remembering that terrible event.

"Good idea. Probably best anyway," Nadia responded.

"You two are pretty close, aren't you?" Jason asked Nadia and her sister.

They both nodded and smiled at the same time when they went to reply to Jason. "Thick as thieves," Nadia said.

"Thicker than blood," Anabella replied.

"Interesting analogies there, ladies," Jason said coyly.

"Do you think Oliver is okay? I hope he didn't get hurt too," Nadia said to the group.

"We'll know soon enough. Nothing we can do about it now."

"Kinda cold reply there, Jason." Donna looked almost sad about the whole situation.

The five of them sat in silence for a while, and then, after what felt like hours, the men returned. Oliver was with them, and he was in tears. When they got settled back inside, Oliver began to speak.

"There wasn't anything I could do. He was dead no matter what I tried. His body was severed in half by one of the ceiling sections that fell on top him. When I made it there, I saw the blood pooling. He had shallow breaths. I tried pushing the concrete off of him but that seemed to make him bleed more."

Oliver had tears in his eyes as he lowered his head into his hands. Everyone let him cry in peace. No one could say anything that would help the situation, so silence was the best option. Finally, once the tears stopped, he looked up at everyone. "When Carter, Carlisle, and Steve came out, they helped me remove the concrete so I could see his body. I guess the block had kept the veins pinched off, so he bled out slower. I think he suffered badly, and there was nothing I could do for my big brother. I just held his hand as he died."

"You did the best you could," Donna said softly.

"Yeah, you did," Nadia reassured.

"But I should have been there with him!"

"Then you would be dead too," Carter said coolly.

"Then I should have made him stay!" Oliver yelled. He stood up and punched the wall. Everyone held their breath as they waited to see if anything would fall from the shock to the structure.

Carlisle stood up beside Oliver and placed his hand onto his shoulder. "Oliver, we are all sorry for your loss, but now isn't the time to cast blame on yourself or second guess what you did or didn't do. Now is the time to honor Charles by living, by helping us get free so your family doesn't have two deaths come home to them."

Oliver shrugged out of Carlisle's shoulder hold and just shook his head back and forth. "Nothing you can say will help me or change how I feel. You just better hope you get us freed before I blame you for his death." He walked off as far as he could in the three feet of room there was and sat down in the corner. Everyone gave him the space he needed while they all sat quietly.

"I did some exploring," Carter stated.

"What did you find?" Anabella perked up and looked over at the man Nadia knew her sister loved.

"I think I have a way to get us out, but it is going to be a lot of work."

"What are the details?" Jason asked Carter.

"There is a little pathway. I think we can haul the broken debris down and clear the path to the outside."

"Where was it at?" Carlisle asked.

Carter picked up his arm, and with his fingers, he pointed to one of the corners. "On the outside wall, a little ways up. We will have to climb about five feet up and then haul the debris out. It is going to be exhausting, and I can't see what it is going to do to the structure of the room and what is already crumbling down."

"Well, it's worth a shot, brother."

"Yes, it is."

"Who are we going to get to haul the debris?" Steve asked.

"That's the other hard part. The hole is so small, the reality is, the men will have a very hard time getting out of it, but the women..." Everyone sucked in a breath as they looked at Nadia, Anabella, and Donna. "Only the girls will get free."

Carter hated that he had to say that. He didn't know what life without Anabella would be like, and he hated to think about it at all, but those were the facts. The hole was going to be big enough for the women only and not the men.

"Never thought it would end like this," he said to Carlisle.

"It still might not."

"Not unless you have some killer plan tucked away you have forgotten to tell me about."

"Don't I always?" Carlisle teased.

"Most of the time, but you and I were very unprepared for this. This is why love is dangerous; it dulls our senses, apparently."

"Stop sounding like the grim reaper, Carter. Have faith. I don't think the girls want us gone just yet. They are smart. They will get help."

"Are you girls ready to start digging? We can take turns. One of the guys can be at the end of the tunnel, helping pull the stuff out, but you guys will have to take turns inside the tunnel, pushing it out towards us."

"I'll go first." Anabella stepped forward and looked at Carter before she climbed up the makeshift steps and settled into the tunnel. She started pulling the debris out and handing it to Carter.

He felt his heart shriveling away looking at her, thinking it could be the last time they ever saw one another. How had things ended up at this point? He had no idea. A year ago, he hadn't even known what love was.

"Hey, Ana?" he said in a whisper.

"Yeah?"

"Before you guys go out of the tunnel, you have to marry me. I won't let you go without knowing you're my wife."

He saw the tears in her eyes. It broke his heart, but he knew she loved him, and this helped solidify it.

"Okay, I will, but who would wed us?"

"Oliver is a minister. He told us that while he was saying prayers over his brother's body. He can have us married in the eyes of the Church, in God's eyes. That's all I'll need. I've already updated my will, naming you the benefactor of everything. I just... I need to marry you now in any way we can before I..." He placed his hand over the left breast pocket of his jacket. He watched her eyes grow big and light up when he made the gesture. He knelt down and bowed his head. "Before I lose you."

"Okay, Carter, I'll marry you and be your wife, but you have to promise me one thing."

"Anything, Ana."

"You won't die."

"Baby, I can't promise that. When you guys get out, we don't know what this tunnel will do to the structure of the room. You've got to get out and save yourselves. And find help."

"Promise you will wait for me to come back then..."

"Of course. I'll always wait for you, now and forever."

"I don't want to go without you. I'm too attached to you, Carter Jackson. You can't leave me!"

Both of their eyes were dripping with tears now. They came together at the top of the makeshift stairs and hugged each other for a long while. In the end, they heard Nadia calling up to them to come down, and so they did.

When they reached the ground, Carter called out to Oliver.

"We need you to marry us, please."

He shook his head back and forth. "I can't. I haven't it in me to marry you. You or anyone."

"That's not an option, Oliver. You will marry us, right now."

He kept shaking his head. "No, Carter, I can't."

Anabella walked past Carter and right up to Oliver. She wrapped her hands around his neck and shoulders and hugged him. After a few seconds, he wrapped his arms around her and returned the hug. They cried together. She cried for the impending loss of Carter. Oliver cried for his brother, and for his own life.

After the two of them embraced long enough to find some comfort in the compassion of a stranger, they released one another. Carter pulled Anabella back towards him and listened to Oliver change his mind.

"Okay, I'll marry you, but only because you hugged me."

Anabella smiled and then hugged Carter and kissed him. "Come on, love. Let's get married."

Nadia and Anabella were talking to each other on one side of the room and looking at Carter and Carlisle. Anabella was nervous for so many reasons. First, she never thought she would want to marry anyone, ever. And second, she was going to lose the only man who had ever come close to giving her this much happiness, and now she was just supposed to be okay with letting it all go by the wayside. How was she going to be able to live with herself? Especially after knowing she was marrying him just to let him die?

"Are you ready, Ana?" Nadia asked.

All she did was nod her head. She looked at the ground and saw the flowers lying on the dinner table. She picked them up and dusted them off. They would have to do. She walked to the makeshift aisle, where Nadia was waiting for her. They locked their arms together and slowly began to walk. When they got to the end, she looked into Carter's eyes and began to cry. Her life was about to be over for good, and she had no way to stop any of it.

Oliver cleared his throat. "Who gives this woman away?"

"I do," Nadia replied firmly.

Anabella stepped closer to Carter, who wrapped his arm around her waist and held her close.

"We come together to die, I mean, to marry these two into holy matrimony. Love is a weird thing. It jumps out of nowhere and bites you on the ass just to then have it ripped away, but if you think about it, all great things get ripped away. The Roman Empire crumbled. The tower of Pisa leans. Even the Twin Towers fell. Everything was meant to end at some point, but what we don't look at is the beginning, and that's what these two have, the beginning. For how long will that beginning last? No one knows, but for now, we come here to celebrate your love."

Anabella had no idea what to think about Oliver's speech. She wanted to cry, to slap him, to scream out at God, but she didn't. She just listened.

"Do you, Anabella, come here freely and of your own free will?"

"I do."

"And do you, Carter, do the same?"

"I do."

"Does someone have some rings?" Oliver's casual tone was starting to annoy Anabella, but if they lived through this, she could redo the marriage any way she wanted and make it proper.

"Here you go." Carlisle leaned over and dropped two rings into Oliver's hands.

Oliver handed one ring to Anabella and said, "Repeat after me."

"Carter, I promise to love you, to honor you, to bring you no shame, to keep your bed warm, to keep your belly full, and to follow you until the end of the earth for as long as we shall live."

After Anabella repeated it, she slid the ring onto Carter's finger.

Oliver then dropped the other ring into Carter's hand, and instead of repeating the same thing she had just said, Carter said what he wanted.

"Anabella, I love you. I love you more now than I could ever imagine loving another human being. I promise, that as long as my heart beats, I will cherish you. I will never forsake you. I will keep you safe, no matter the cost to myself, and I will always hold your love as the most precious gift ever given to me. With this ring, I promise you my soul, for an eternity."

As he slid the ring on Anabella's finger, she cried. Her whole body was shaking as she let the tears fall down her cheeks.

"That was very sweet. Not what I said to repeat, but sweet," Oliver said. "So does anyone present feel that these two should not get married? If so, speak now, or forever be peaceful."

A few seconds of silence passed, and then Oliver continued. "By the powers vested in me, I now proclaim you Mr. and Mrs. Carter..." He paused. "What is your last name?"

"Jackson!" Nadia, Anabella, Carter, and Carlisle all shouted.

"Okay, okay, I now proclaim you Mr. and Mrs. Carter Jackson. You may kiss your bride."

Carter pulled her close to him and kissed her, hard and passionate. He reached over, lifted her into his arms, and carried her down the makeshift aisle and into the safe zone. No one dared to follow them. He closed the cloth door and looked deep into her eyes.

"Thank you for this."

"It was no problem."

"You have no idea how much I love you, Ana."

"It's Mrs. Jackson to you, sir."

"My deepest apologies. You have no idea how much I love you, Mrs. Jackson."

"Mom and Dad are going to hate that they missed it."

"We can do another ceremony when we all get home."

They both let their voices drop silent at that thought. Home. There was no telling how that was going to happen or when, but she had to be hopeful.

"I'm not ready to leave you," she told him.

"Same here."

"So how are we going to make this work? Maybe I can just stay with you, and Nadia can go get help with Donna."

Carter shook his head back and forth. "No, you need to live. No matter what, you must live, or I'll be a failure."

"Kiss me, Carter," she requested.

And he kissed her. He let his tongue travel through her mouth, circling and teasing. He felt so good on top of her, his body pressed to hers. She loved it. She loved him with all of her soul. The two of them spent the next hour worshipping their love, their one and only time as husband and wife. She would cherish the memory for the rest of her life. She would have no choice. It was the one thing she couldn't change, because the hole to escape was too small.

So she would just enjoy this.

Once they were ready, they left the seclusion of the safe area, and everyone applauded when they came out. Anabella felt her face flush a deep red and saw her sister grin from ear to ear. Maybe it was a good thing that even in a moment of severe loss and tragedy she found someone smiling because of her and Carter. She walked up to Nadia and gave her a hug. She didn't want to let go of her little sister. She wanted to stay in this moment forever.

"It's time to go, Ana. The tunnel is ready." She heard Carter's voice behind her, and the tears started again.

CHAPTER TEN

The girls pushed through the last bit of the rubble and came out just outside of the building. There were people all around them. Emergency first responders rushed over to the building to assist the women in their escape. The commotion was nonstop. Everywhere they looked, there were police officers and firemen. The medical personnel came over to check out each of the ladies. They took their blood pressure and gave a quick triage to each one. The only problem was none of the first responders spoke English. The women were frantically trying to communicate with someone to tell them there were still more people trapped inside.

"Mrs. Ali!" someone yelled from across the way. "Ms. Maverick!"

Anabella and Nadia both turned around to see the resort manager running towards them.

"Where are the men? Are they still alive?" he asked.

Nadia and Anabella began to tell him everything that had happened and where the others were. Within an hour they had construction equipment delivered to the resort site, including a large green excavator. The bucket had eight sharp teeth and was about four feet wide. Nadia had never seen a piece of equipment so large. She and Anabella held each other tightly as the arm reached out and started to scrape away at the rubble. They had to take the progress slow. There was the worry that the building would collapse more than it already had if they removed too much of the rubble too quickly.

"They will be okay, Ana. They are going to get to them in time."

"I hope so. We don't even know if what they are doing has caused more damage."

"Look at those large concrete blocks. I can't believe how much rebar is in them and how huge they are."

They both looked over their shoulders and watched Donna pacing up and down the sidewalk, crying. Neither of them had thought to offer her comfort. Casey was in there too. All three of them had people they loved inside.

Nadia and Anabella both walked over to Donna and wrapped their arms around her. The three of them stayed huddled together in that same position, waiting on news of the men.

"Ana!"

"Donna!"

The voices could be heard through all the commotion. Nadia watched as her sister and Donna ran over to their men. Her heart fell from her chest to her stomach. She stared as Anabella and Carter embraced, kissing each other. Next, Jason and Oliver came walking out. Where was Carlisle?

Seconds turned into minutes. Life was crumbling as each moment ticked by. She could hear her heart beating, felt it all over her body. She didn't even realize her feet were running. She was moving toward the rubble, screaming.

"Carlisle! Carlisle!"

She was screaming into an empty pile of concrete. She jumped over the rebar that was lying along the ground. She stepped onto the chunks of concrete and bounced from one to the next until she was at the entrance that the excavator had made.

With tears rolling down her cheeks she screamed out again, "Carlisle!" She couldn't see into the black. The emergency lighting was no longer on. All that was before her face was dust and dirt. She dropped to her knees with her hands on her face, crying. She kept repeating his name over and over. It was never ending to her. The worst nightmare she could ever encounter was happening. She was losing her grip on reality.

Their child was going to grow up without a father, and it was all because she was cursed by some crazy spiritual being to have disasters happen to those she loved.

"Nadia?" The voice was faint, but it was there. She wasn't imagining it. She moved her head up and looked out. Inside the rubble were two men, one walking, one in the other's arms.

"He's alive…" she said out loud to herself. She was quick to get onto her feet, and as the figures came closer, she saw him, Carlisle, carrying Steve out of the pits of darkness.

She moved towards them as Carlisle set Steve down on a block of concrete just in time to catch Nadia as she jumped into his arms.

"Don't ever do that to me again!" she yelled at him right before she kissed him. His arms held onto her tightly, and he began to stroke her hair and back in an attempt to calm her down.

"Shh, my pet, you know I would never leave you."

"You scared the hell out of me, Carlisle. I can't believe you did that!"

He lifted her up off of her feet and held her close to his chest while he carried them down to safety. When they reached Carter and Anabella, Nadia had stopped crying. Everyone except Charles had made it out alive.

Donna looked around and said, "Hey, we never did find the murder."

"It was Nadia," Anabella said.

"Hey, how did you know?" Nadia said in a shocked voice.

"Your footprint. I saw it in the dirt."

Nadia shook her head back and forth. "No way…"

Carter elbowed Nadia gently and smiled. "Sorry, kid, she did. We talked about it."

"Well damn, I thought I was going to be able to fool everyone."

"If it makes you feel any better, you fooled us," Steve said, smiling at Nadia.

She grinned back at him. "Yeah, that does help."

"Who's ready to go home?" Carter asked.

"I think we all are." Carlisle looked down at Nadia. "Aren't you?"

She nodded her head and then reached a hand out to Donna. "It was very nice to meet you, all of you guys. Hope you have safe trips home." She turned to Oliver and began to walk towards him. "I am extremely sorry for your brother. I wish there was a way it could have happened differently."

All Oliver did was nod his head.

Nadia watched Carter walk off in the direction of the resort manager. Anabella and Carlisle came up to her, and as a family, they all walked away from the rubble and into the parking lot where their rental car was located. Carter joined them a few minutes later and got into the passenger seat.

"He is issuing a refund for the hotel expenses that we already paid to help compensate for our lost belongings."

"It's sad that we won't even have any collectibles to remember the trip by," Anabella said.

Everyone in the car turned and looked at her. Their faces didn't have shock on them but a bit of disbelief. Nadia was the first to speak. "Do you really want to remember this trip?"

Anabella gave a simple nod. "Yes. I got married here."

"You're right. We did. Let us go get you something to remember it by," Carter said in a very loving tone.

The four of them drove into the local shop. They got out of the vehicle and started walking up and down the little shops of handmade jewelry. There was a two piece set necklace that caught both women's eye. They were circle based necklace, tan, made of some type of leather material. One piece had a base design in green colors and one based in red colors. The beads on each had circular shapes on them. The beads were made to look like a sun with mixed but matching colors.

"This is very different," Anabella said to Nadia.

"It is. It's like they match, but they are unique too. They give off a very 'African' vibe."

"Unique, much like you two sisters," Carlisle said with a smile on his face. He reached into his pocket and pulled out his wallet. He of course always carried cash on him in the currency of the country. He paid for both necklaces, and then they were on their way to the airport.

"I've kept our plane on standby the entire trip, so she will be ready at the airfield. I'm also glad I left all of our passports with them in their safe on the plane." Carter seemed quite proud of himself as he spoke.

"Yes, always the planner, you are," Anabella teased.

"Always be prepared. That's my motto."

"Since when are you a boy scout?" Nadia asked jokingly.

"I was the original boy scout."

"Doubtful, I'm older than you, and I taught you everything you know, so I must be the original." Carlisle laughed as he teased Carter.

"Can't we all just get along?" Anabella sighed and let out a yawn.

"I think we are all just tired. Thank god the private plane has a shower and sink so we can clean up."

"They have more than that, Ana. They also have a change of clothes for everyone and food."

"What are we waiting for then, husband? Get us to that plane!"

Going home from Africa was hard for Carter. He had the coordinates to stop in Cedar Rapids, but he really wanted to just take Anabella back to Houston with him. He was looking forward to being able to start their life together, the two of them, but he knew the Mavericks were very liberal in some senses and very traditional in others. His worry was that Kain wouldn't approve of what had happened, and Kain had such a huge impact on the Maverick women.

He didn't quite understand the relationship the brother and sisters shared. It seemed almost like the three of them cared about each other's opinions more than those of their parents. Sometimes he had issues with understanding typical human emotions. People like him and Carlisle grew up fending for themselves for so long and relying only on their own skills, that often times it caused problems when they added non-assassin counterparts into their lives.

But he had watched Carlisle and Nadia make it work over the past year, and he was anxious to make it work with Anabella. They had worked out an easy arrangement thus far. He would be okay if they kept it up, to an extent. He of course would want more time in Houston. Carter was willing to work out those details later.

"How much longer do we have on the flight?" Anabella asked him as she rolled over in her seat and rested her head on his shoulder.

"We should be landing in about five minutes. I haven't called anyone to tell them we're coming in, so we should probably just go back to your place."

"That sounds good. Is a car service going to pick us up?"

"Yes, Carlisle took care of that already." He watched her stretch her arms out, working out her stiff muscles from the long flight home.

"Next time we go on a vacation, I want to do a simple cruise. Nothing drastic and crazy."

"Whatever you want, Mrs. Jackson. We still have a honeymoon to plan and take."

She yawned again and nodded her head. "We do. Mom's going to be sad she missed the wedding."

"Do you want to pretend it didn't happen and do it again?"

Anabella thought about this for a while before she answered, shaking her head no. "It's okay. She saw Nadia and Kain. Someone has to be different, right?"

"Okay, as long as you're happy, that's all that matters."

"Thank you, Carter, for loving me." She leaned in, placed her lips on his, and let her love overflow.

He wished it was just the two of them on the plane so they could bond properly as a married couple, but he would soon have her alone, and that was what mattered. What happened later was what he was looking forward to the most.

"When will you want to go back to Houston?"

"Once you are ready. I'm sure you will need to pack a few things to bring down since it will be your permanent home."

He watched her face as he said that and saw she wasn't exactly pleased.

"I know that's what you want, Carter, but my life is in Iowa."

"For now it is, but eventually it will migrate to Houston. Especially once we have children."

"You want children?" she said in a sort of breathless tone.

"Of course. You and I will make fantastic looking children. We can't deprive the world of that kind of beauty."

The look on her face, the smile, after he said that, warmed him to the bone.

"This is your captain speaking. We are approaching the airfield. Please buckle up and secure your belongings. We will be touching down shortly."

The intercom announcement distracted him from his thoughts and made him focus on the present. The nose of the plane dropped lower, and shortly after, the plane was landing at the airport. Carlisle had requested two cars to pick them up from the airstrip. He was grateful that Carlisle had thought that far ahead.

Major airports were complicated and chaotic, like the ones in Dallas and Houston. The Eastern Iowa Airport, however, always made it easy for his pilot to land. He remembered one time when he had landed at the Dallas airport, it had taken him one hour to leave his private plane and make it to a vehicle. Getting through the crowd and check points had taken a lot of patience. It was so bad in Houston that Carter had actually started using Hooks airport, a small private field in the middle of Spring, just north of town.

It was late at night when they touched down, and by the time they got into their chartered cars to head home, it was close to midnight. They got on Wright Brothers Boulevard and headed towards interstate 380 before turning towards town. They traveled for about fifteen minutes, and when Carter and Anabella pulled up to her home, they both gave a sigh of relief that the adventure was over.

"Well, most of it was a nice trip," Anabella said while she poured them glasses of wine.

"If by most you mean everything except the last thirty-six hours, yes."

Carter took a wine glass from her and lifted it up in the air. "To us, Mrs. Jackson. May you feel nothing but happiness and love for the rest of your life."

"I'll drink that." She clinked her glass to his, and then they both drank.

An idea hit Carter like a ton of bricks and he set the glass down and looked very seriously into Anabella's eyes. "I've made a mistake. Come with me, quick!" He pulled her to the front door, opened it, and shoed her outside.

"What's wrong? What happened?"

"I forgot to carry you over the threshold!" He leaned over, swept her legs up into his arms, walked through the underpass of the open door, and then let her feet back down to the ground. "I hope I didn't just jinx us!"

"Superstitions only work if you put faith into them. And besides, Mom and Dad own this place, not me. I may live here, but I never bought it. So it isn't like this is my home. It's just where I keep my change of clothes. We can do it right when we get to your house, since that will be our home."

He nodded and smiled. "I like how you think. See, we are already a good team."

"We were always a good team. What are you talking about?!"

"I know, love. Shall we go to bed? You look tired, and I feel like a train ran me over."

Anabella smiled and nodded, then grabbed his hand and led him back to through the house to her bedroom, where she could finally go to sleep in peace after the chaos they had just experienced.

Carlisle held Nadia close to him so that when she woke up at 5:45 a.m. he didn't let her get out of bed. "Only you would wake up at exactly the same time after a vacation. You would think with jet lag and exhaustion you would sleep in until at least seven."

"I can't help it; my mental clock has a way of just knowing it is time to wake up."

"You're not getting out of bed. You're staying right here. You need your sleep."

"We need our sleep, Mr. A. Don't worry. I am not moving one muscle."

"Good, because I like you in my arms."

"I like being held in your arms too, so it works."

The two of them let the silence take over for a few minutes before Nadia spoke again. "I was scared I'd lost you for real this time."

"I know you were, my pet, but you know I would never leave you."

"It felt so real, so traumatizing."

He leaned over and kissed the back of her neck as he held her in his arms. "I promise, Nadia, I'm not going anywhere."

She let her fingers run up and down his arms and just nodded into her pillow. He hoped she would be able to fall back to sleep. The whole vacation had been a messed up situation, and he knew she would need some time to recover from it.

Once she was back asleep, he slipped her out of his arms and tucked her back into bed. He made his way down the hall and into his computer room to check on a few situations that he had left festering before the vacation. He turned on his laptop and began sifting through all the emails he had missed.

There was one in particular that he found interesting. Through his network of brothers, he had been notified that a criminal from Des Moines was found not guilty because the police had botched something. Carlisle hated technicalities. He looked at his watch and saw that, if he left now, he could be in Des Moines by eight and then back to Nadia by eleven at the latest. Hopefully she would stay asleep until then. It had been a long journey, and she needed her rest.

He couldn't just leave. He would have to let her know, so he went back into the bedroom and gently woke her up. "My pet, I am going to get a jump on the day and start replacing the items we lost on the trip. I'll be back before lunch."

Nadia mumbled a response, half asleep, and he took that as understanding from her. He kissed the top of her head and then walked out of the bedroom and into the closet to get ready for his trip.

CHAPTER ELEVEN

Death wasn't something that Carlisle took lightly. It was a necessary evil that he had no choice but to execute. Being a hero wasn't doing the things that the general population liked; it was doing things that the general population knew were necessary but didn't have the ability to do themselves. That's how reality was. Whether or not people wanted to admit that was a different story.

The first few lives he'd had to take had not necessarily hard on him. He remembered being nervous, but it had been more like the nervousness one got when approaching a new job or a new class for school. He'd known that he could carry out the act, because he believed in the cause. He believed in the reasons behind everything.

What he didn't believe in was letting evil roam the earth and not doing anything about to put an end to the death and destruction. Often times, when people spoke about him and he heard the whispers in the wind about something he may or may not have done, he found the humor in the common person's understanding of what his psyche was. Words like sociopath and psychopath were thrown around. While he didn't like his associates calling him those things, he did find humor in it. He found it laughable because he could do what they couldn't, and he still managed to sleep at night. How was it that being of an above average intelligence with the moral ability to do the things that the common people couldn't meant he should be labeled with such words? That was something that always fascinated him and likewise his brothers-in-arms.

In Carlisle's, world there was more than just himself and Carter. There was a brotherhood, one that reached far and wide in a vast array of places with contacts everywhere. It was similar to the newest Batman movies, with Bruce Wane being trained by Ra's al Ghul. Even though that wasn't exactly what happened in the comics, it made sense and correlated very well with what his own brotherhood's beliefs. Sometimes he wanted to write a paper comparing the fiction and the reality, the cinematic brotherhood versus the real brotherhood. However, the last thing Mafdet wanted or needed was scholars investigating ways to pervert the system and lifestyle.

Because of that, he was left to ponder these types of things on his own or with Carter and the other one or two men who he'd chosen to let himself grow close to, like Tavin.

The same individual who had made him aware of this current assignment had been in this business for three years, still a rookie for all intents and purposes, but an asset to have in one's corner nonetheless. The difference between this rookie and the other brothers was that he had family who was still alive. It had almost always been a requirement, no family before entering the cryptic society. That way there were no potential casualties for one's own errors, but as he looked at his own life, Carlisle realized those rules seemed to bend now more than ever before.

Tavin had a sister. Both of them had grown up in the foster care system in America, in which children either find that forever home or they age out of the system and are left to fend for themselves. Carlisle's mentor and sponsor though the program, Abraham, had found Tavin and his sister Sasha wandering the streets of Denver one Thursday night. The two were twins, and because of that, they stuck together pretty closely.

At first, Carlisle had been skeptical about bringing two twenty-year-olds into his life. He remembered himself at that age. It had been a cocky son of a bitch that his now forty something self would hardly be able to stand, but Carlisle had trusted Abraham from the beginning and helped to train Tavin.

For eight months, the three of them had spent all day and night together, training, eating, and sleeping. Tavin's sister was sent to a boarding school where Abraham saw to it her education was finished and that she was able to conduct business with the elite society of the world. The bad habits she had learned from the streets were extinguished from her mannerisms.

Now, almost two and a half years after Tavin's training had been completed, he was an asset assigned to northwest part of the country. He was based out of Oregon, but his sister lived in Wyoming. Sasha and Tavin still kept in contact with Carlisle and with Carter on a regular basis. Carlisle always thought Sasha was bound to set her hooks into Carter, but he was extremely happy that Anabella had come along when she had. As much as the young girl had become an acceptable part of his life when dealing with Tavin, he wasn't sure he would be able to take her as a permanent part of his normalcy. But then again, there were very few women he could tolerate.

The article that Tavin had sent Carlisle stated that the, now acquitted, Rob Feldnich, had faced a felony charge of indecency with a minor and attempted assault against a man in a bar. He was quite interested in how the two charges worked together, as they didn't seem to go hand in hand, so on his drive to Des Moines, he started to listen to different news reports he could find regarding Mr. Feldnich.

After making his way across the state line, he had heard all he needed to about this man. After causing a bar fight and losing it in the middle of the day, he'd gone home and found one of the neighborhood dogs urinating on the side of the building and joined him. Unfortunately for this man, that building was the neighborhood school. The element that allowed him to be found not guilty of these charges was that the individual who had seen him relieving himself was a child who later had trouble identifying him during a line-up. Normally, this kind of case wasn't one that would warrant attention from Mafdet's brotherhood, so he placed a call in to his source.

The phone rang a few times, and then a male voice picked up on the other end. "Mr. A, it's good to hear from you, sir."

"Hello, Tavin. I assume you are well," he politely responded.

"I am. Thank you for asking. How is married life?"

"Better now that we are home. I have been studying up on the file you sent me, and I'm unsure why this man is worthy of my time."

"Did you see the attachment?"

"No, I did not."

"Did you not see my new signature with the image of the Denver Broncos on it?"

"Well that I saw. What about it?"

"You were supposed to download the encryption."

"As you left no instructions to do so, how was I supposed to know?"

"Aren't you the computer genius?" Tavin replied sarcastically.

"Tavin, I do not have all day. Just tell me what you failed to tell me in your email."

"Okay. I started to ignore this article when I first saw it, but then the name sounded so familiar, so I ran some scans through police records and some other databases, and this guy has actually been questioned and a person of interest in nine unsolved murders."

"Can you prove it is him?" Carlisle's tone became more serious, and his appreciation of Tavin's keen senses came back to the forefront of his mind.

"No, he's had an unconfirmed alibi with each incident."

"And what is that?"

"He's home alone in the hotel room ordering room service or some pay per view movie, which is easy enough to make happen; just pay someone to be in there at that time."

Carlisle listened to Tavin speak for another minute, and then he remained silent. "A, you there?" Tavin's voice said through the speaker of the car audio system.

"Yeah, T, I'm here. I'm just thinking about this guy. I usually like to have more evidence and hardcore facts before I go after someone."

"I've talked about it with Abraham. He agreed."

Carlisle let his fingers strum along the steering wheel while he drove along the highway. He wasn't typically this conflicted, especially when it was a sanctioned hit, but this time was different. He initiated his turn indicator on, began to move across the lanes of the highway, and exited the road. He made a U-turn and got back on the highway, this time going in the direction of home.

"Sorry, Tavin. I usually accept your gut, especially when our mentor is backing you, but this time I think I am going to simply go rejoin my wife in our bed and keep my hands clean of this one. If you want it, take it, but I'm out."

"If that's how you feel, Mr. A."

"It is."

"Do you want me to stop by when I pass through town?"

"Yes, actually, I do. Mr. J had an eventful trip abroad, and we are going to be having a celebration. I'll send you more details, but needless to say, there is a new member of our brotherhood family you need to meet. Now is as good a time as any."

He let the line go dead after that. Maybe he was turning soft in his old age, or his married life, but he had made a promise to himself when he had first started this over three decades ago. He would never kill anyone who he did not honestly feel deserved it, and with this guy, he just couldn't swear on his life that he did. Each time his hands were the cause of death, each time he took a life, he had better be able to swear on his own that it was justified.

On his way back in Cedar Rapids, Carlisle made a few phone calls to a personal stylist at the mall. He gave Nadia's and his sizes and a description of the clothing they had lost and was assured that new items would be awaiting him once he arrived at the mall. People had an image of Cedar Rapids as some sticks village with no culture. What the masses didn't understand was, no matter where you were, money could and did buy you anything you needed. Just because the mass populace didn't know it was available, didn't mean it wasn't.

He made it to the mall in good time and then quickly met up with Amber, the shopping assistant. They exchanged the clothes and money, and then, after tucking them in his car, he drove home to Nadia. It was during the last block of the trip when his phone started to ring, and he saw Nadia's name flash across his cell phone.

"Hey, you," he said after he answered.

"Hey, yourself. Thought you would be home by now."

"So did I, but I got caught at the mall."

"Doing?"

"Shopping. What else does one do at the mall?" he teased, not wanting her to know the truth just yet.

"In your line of work, Carlisle, anything is possible. When will you be home?" she asked.

"Before you can get out of bed, whip up some French toast, and pour us a glass of milk."

"Wanna make a bet on that, hotshot?" she toyed back at him.

"Oh, you're on, my pet."

"Good, loser cleans the house for a month." After that, Carlisle heard silence. Nadia had ended the call right as he pulled into the driveway.

He reached into his car and removed the bags of clothes. He was excited to surprise her with a new necklace. No, she hadn't lost one in Africa, but when he'd been running through the list of clothes she needed replaced, it had seemed like a good idea to make sure she had matching jewelry to go with at least one of the new dresses and shoes.

When Carlisle walked into the house, his mouth dropped open. There his wife stood in nothing but an apron, grinning ear to ear. The table had been set, and on top of it was French toast, milk, orange juice, and sliced fruit and cheeses. Sometimes it worried him how well she knew him.

"You're a witch," he said, grinning at her.

"Maybe." She beamed. "Or maybe I have learned a thing or two from my husband over the past year."

"A thing or two? Looks like you have learned more than a thing or two." He placed all of the bags on the couch and walked over to her. He wrapped his arms around her waist and pulled her close. "Mrs. Ali, are you naked under there?"

She simply nodded.

"I give. You're the master. You have it all figured out."

A couple hours later, Nadia and Carlisle were snuggling on the couch, listening to the crackling fireplace, and watching The Twilight Zone. They were both feeling content, and Nadia felt like things could get back to normal.

"I think we need to be careful who we travel with next time."

Carlisle looked up and gave her a smirk. "You think it was your sister who jinxed us?"

"Well, let us look at the facts." Nadia pushed off of him and sat up, her back straight as a board and her shoulders shrugged back with confidence.

"Okay, hit me with it."

"First," she smiled and held up a finger, "we all go to Houston, and what happens?"

"You get kidnapped."

"Exactly." She then paused and raised her second finger up. "We go to Africa and what happens?"

"We almost die."

"And what do both of these events all have in common?"

"All four of us were together?"

"No! I mean, yes, but no! Ana had doubts about both trips, and her doubts turned into realities."

"Your sister thought you would get kidnapped and then thought we all would get trapped with an earthquake?" He paused. "Those are some damn good psychic powers there."

"No, she just thought something bad would happen."

"And you are arguing that, if she hadn't brought any negativity up at all, that none of it would have happened."

"I'm glad you understand my point."

"Honey," Carlisle said in a placating tone, "I don't think it works like that."

"You don't know. It might, karma and all."

He shook his head a couple times. "Karma doesn't work like that. Karma is if you do bad things in this world, then bad things will happen to you."

"You're an assassin, and look at you. You don't have bad things happen to you." She paused. "So how is that for your karma theory?"

"There's a difference. I live by a code. I don't kill at random, and you know that. The code is there to protect people, which is what I do."

"Feels a little hypocritical if you ask me, but karma, she is a—"

He cut her off with a quick kiss and then placed his index finger along her jawline and pushed her head slightly towards the television. Carlisle picked up the remote and started flipping through the channels until he landed on the news. They watched the news anchor talk about the lead story. Carlisle stayed silent while the broadcaster spoke, and once it was over, he turned the television to mute and looked at his wife.

"You see that news broadcast?"

She felt him watching her as she nodded his head.

"I know I don't talk about what I do much, but that's who I was assigned to this morning."

"The man on the news?"

"No, well, yes. The man the news is about. I was assigned to terminate him."

"And you didn't? Tell me about him."

"What do you want to know?" he said calmly.

"What he did to warrant being assigned to you. I assume it was something bad."

Carlisle shrugged. Nadia wasn't used to seeing uncertainty in his eyes. That made her worry some. "That's just it. I don't know that he did anything, exactly." He went into the few details he knew about the case.

This was the first time he had really included her in his work, in his cases. She knew what the essentials involved were, but hearing the why behind everything, more importantly, the reason behind why he turned the job down, was important to Nadia. It showed her that he wasn't just a killer. He was what he had always claimed to be, the hand of justice.

"What are you thinking, my pet?"

She tapped her finger to her lip a few times then smiled. "I think I am more glad I married you every day, Mr. Ali."

"All because I didn't complete the job?"

"No."

"Then why?"

"All because you stuck to your morals, because you're not a fake."

"Wouldn't you expect me to do that?"

"Of course! But sometimes it is just nice to see the thing you always suspected to be true, actually coming true."

He pulled her into him and held her close. She could hear his heartbeat echoing in her ear. She placed her hand over his heart and let the pulses shimmer through her palm. They sat here and listened as the news anchor switched to the weather and the sunny skies that they were in for during the upcoming weekend.

"Nadia?" He said her name with such a purr every time that it made her body shiver with excitement and fear simultaneously.

"Yeah?"

"What did you do with all that money you won from the lottery?"

This question startled her. She and he had never spoken about that, and it had happened so many years back that she hardly thought of it now. "I made investments."

"What kind?"

"The kind that pay back over time." She leaned in and kissed him while pushing his back down to the couch, quieting any further comments until they were both ready to join the world again.

CHAPTER TWELVE

Telling your parents you had run off and gotten married was never easy, especially when your mother was Laura Maverick, but that was exactly what Anabella had been working herself up to doing. She had been sitting in her parents' driveway for fifteen minutes now. Carter was in the driver's seat next to her, laughing and shaking his head.

"Something funny over there?"

"You," he said in a playful jab.

"I fail to see the humor in this situation, Mr. Jackson. In fact, this is entirely your fault, and I am going to be sure to let them know it!"

"Come on. You can't be serious, Ana! How old are you? And you're scared of your mother?" He shook his head back and forth at her while smiling ear to ear.

"You don't know her very well yet, Carter. You'll see. She will give you that look, and then you will know she has your goose cooked."

"I have seen her off and on for the last year since Nadia's wedding. You don't think I know your family after all that time?" He turned the key in the ignition to the off position. "We're getting out of the car, come on."

"Don't say I didn't warn you. Dad may be upset too. He's always the toss up."

Carlisle had told Carter about her family. Anabella had heard him. But she didn't know if Carter really knew what they were like. Over the last year, the time he had been around had been limited, and everyone was always on their best behavior. That was how it worked. When guests were around, no one acted crazy. This was what scared Anabella. Now he wasn't a guest; he was family, and the full weight of the Maverick clan was about to come crashing down on him.

As they approached the house, Anabella noticed the curtains on the front window moving. Great, someone had been watching. Her stomach had butterflies as she walked up the two steps and knocked on the front door. There wasn't a moment's pause before the door swung open and a little toothless boy was smiling up at her with his arms stretched wide open.

"Aunt Ana!" Daman's voice shrieked in excitement as he threw himself on her, engulfing her in his love. He smelled of candy and dirt, two of her favorite smells.

"Hey, little man, did you miss me?"

He nodded his head vigorously up and down. Then he opened his mouth and pointed with his finger to his front two teeth. "Notice anything, Aunt Ana?" he mumbled out while exposing his mouth to the air.

"Oh my, look at you! You're toothless! I bet you loved what the tooth fairy left you!" She knelt down and pulled his shirt down around his waist and then tousled his hair. She watched his happy expression grow brighter as he began to tell her how he had received five dollars for each tooth he had lost.

"Where is Grandma?" she asked as she stood back up with the help of Carter's extended hand.

"I'm right here, honey," Laura called from the kitchen. "Come in here. I'm sure you are hungry after your long trip."

"Mom, I've eaten since I got back, but I'll be glad to nibble on whatever you are cooking."

"Be sure to bring that boy of yours back here. I'm sure he needs nourishment too."

Laura Maverick always knew what was going on, even if she couldn't see it at the exact moment it was playing out. The fact that she knew Carter had been with her was eerie but comforting in some ways.

"Let's get this over with," she said to Carter.

"After you, ma'am."

"Get what's over?" Daman asked her while they all walked into the kitchen.

"Nothing, sweetie. Why don't you go play?"

"I gots no one to play wiff. Leon's with Dad." Daman lowered his head, trying to act like he was sad, but everyone knew he was joking.

"I'll go play with you," Carter suggested. He knelt down and started to talk to Daman at his own eye level.

"Wiff you?! Okay, I'll go get a ball! Be right back." Like the Tasmanian Devil, Daman ran out of the kitchen, leaving a trail of dust, and quickly hurried back. He grabbed onto Carter's hand and led him out to the back yard where they began to toss the football back and forth.

"You have a telling smile on your face there, my daughter."

"Do I?" Anabella said in a lowered tone.

"Yes, you do. Want to tell me what is causing that large grin?"

"Him," Anabella replied.

"Obviously, but what about him?" Laura walked over to her daughter and handed her a slice of apple pie. It was warm, fresh out of the oven, with sugar crystals sprinkled along the top of it. There was nothing like her mom's home cooked apple pie.

"Don't be mad, Mom."

"Are you happy?" Laura asked.

"Yes, I am."

"Then I'll never be mad if you're happy." She sat down at the table and started eating her own piece of pie. "Tell me everything."

There was something about mothers and how they were able to drag information out of their children with virtually no effort. Anabella often thought that the government should gather up the toughest mothers and have them teach interviewing tactics. It was an art, a skill that some possessed more than others. Laura Maverick was one of the better ones, mainly because she served pie with her interrogations.

After ten minutes of her mother sitting quietly and Anabella retelling everything that had happened in Africa, they sat there in silence, just looking at one another. Laura was the first to speak. Anabella was scared about what she was about to hear.

"Now I have two assassin son-in-laws. Is that what you are telling me?"

"You don't have to focus on that part, Mom."

"I kind of do. I have to think about your safety. I've already resigned myself to the fact Nadia is a hopeless mess, and Carlisle will have a lifetime of trying to keep tabs on her, but you… You've always been the levelheaded one of the two. I just want to make sure that isn't changing is all."

"No, it isn't changing. Nadia will always be the troublemaker."

The two women laughed, and once their pie was finished, they stood up. Anabella watched as her mother's gaze shifted off of her and to the back yard where Carter was tossing the football with Daman. "He is a handsome man."

"Yes, he is."

"He will give me very good looking grandchildren."

"Mom! Is that all you care about?"

"No, but it is something that is extremely important."

Anabella picked up a dishcloth that was sitting on the tabletop and tossed it at her mother's head. "You're horrible, Mom!"

"Me? You're the one who went off and got married without us. I would like to think you're the horrible one, young lady. Just be glad I forgive you."

"I love you, Mom."

"I love you too, Anabella."

The two women hugged out the rest of the unsaid words before they heard the front door open. Anabella's dad's presence was always powerful, but for some reason, today, it was more so than normal.

"Well, if that isn't the best sight to see for an old man walking into his home, two of his three favorite women hugging and the smell of apple pie!"

Laura and Anabella looked over their shoulders at William as he walked through the threshold of the kitchen. "Care if I get in on this family moment?" he teased.

The women both opened their arms, and William stepped forward into their embrace. Anabella loved this most about her parents, the amount of love they had for their children.

Daman and Carter opened the back door and walked inside. Carter's voice rang through Anabella's ears as his next comment sank her heart into her chest.

"I told you they weren't going to be mad that we got married!"

Anabella could hear the happiness in her now husband's voice, and she felt her father's arm tense around her as the news hit him for the first time. She looked up at her dad and smiled as best as she could as he pulled away from her.

"Married?"

"You didn't tell them?" Carter questioned.

Anabella turned her head towards him. "I told Mom! Dad just got home."

"Oh shit," Carter said in a low moan.

"You said a potty word!" Daman yelled. "Fifty cents into the jar." He pointed to the jar sitting on the television.

"William, I'm sorry. I thought she'd told you." Carter stepped closer to Anabella and wrapped his arm around her waist. She waited for the outburst her father was entitled to, but nothing came. He simply moved his eyes up and down over Carter's body as if inspecting him.

"Ana told me everything that happened, William… There is a good reason for it," her mother said, stepping in.

William turned his head towards his wife and spoke. "I would have to assume the 'good reason' is that he loves her, otherwise nothing else would be acceptable."

"I do love her!" Carter quickly stated.

"Good to know, but you didn't ask my permission," William said.

"There wasn't really the time, Papa," Anabella explained. "It was sort of a life or death situation."

"Why don't we just all sit down? I'll get more pie, and you two kids can tell him all about it."

"I wanna hear too. I never get included." Daman's face looked like he might burst into tears if he wasn't included.

Anabella watched as Carter leaned down, picked up her nephew, and held him close. "I'll tell you what. How about I tell you what happened, and your granddad can simply listen."

"Wow, like an adult!" Daman proclaimed.

That broke the ice and made all of them laugh. "Yes, like an adult," Carter replied.

For the second time that day, Anabella nibbled away on apple pie and explained about the earthquake and the near death experience they all had encountered. By the end of the story, William was okay with their marriage, and Laura had found a way to shove more sugar down their systems than either of them had eaten in months.

Dinner that night had been deemed a family affair, and everyone showed up, Kain, Nadia, Carlisle, the boys, and Anabella's parents. Carter had spent many evenings with these people, but never as the center of attention. That had always been Carlisle. Now it was his turn, he supposed. He would have given anything to have had a family like this when he was growing up. Maybe that would have made his life different, and he wouldn't have ended up going through all of the things he had, but then he wouldn't have Anabella.

"You look deep in thought there, brother." Carlisle walked up to him and handed him a longneck bottle of beer.

"Always quick to notice the obvious, aren't you?"

"That's why I get paid the big bucks."

The two men clinked their drinks together in a mock cheers and sat down outside in the back yard on the swing set. There wasn't much dialogue between the two of them. It wasn't needed. They had been brothers in arms for years, and now they were brothers. No one would know these two better than the two of them themselves, and that was comforting in some ways to Carter. Carlisle had helped him out of life and death situations more than once and owed him everything.

"You ever think about what we would have been like had we been part of a family like this?" He looked at Carlisle with the most sincere and heartfelt expression.

"Course I do, but what happens to us, happens for a reason."

"I know that's what we all say we believe, but the reality is, we were dealt a shit hand."

"I disagree," Carlisle said coolly.

"How do you disagree?"

"You know, we wouldn't have the Mavericks now had we grown up with a family like them. It was meant to happen this way. It was for the best. Our goddess protected us when we needed it, and here we are."

"And here we are."

They both took drinks from their beers and swung on the swing for a few moments in silent thought.

"Had something happen today," Carlisle finally said.

"What kind of something?"

"Nothing major, at least, I don't think it is. Tavin contacted me about a case."

"I haven't spoken to him in a while. How are he and his sister?"

"From what I could tell, they are fine." Carlisle took another drink, and then spoke. "He gave me someone that he and Abraham have been watching."

"Did something happen when you went to work?"

"No, but only because I declined it. Just didn't feel on the up and up."

"You don't think Tavin was doing something under the table, do you?"

"No, I spoke to him. He was sure of what he sent me."

"Then what's the issue, Carlisle?"

"I don't know, just a gut feeling I had. Felt like Abraham was being sloppy or something."

Carter laughed, took a drink, and said, "He is getting old. It was bound to happen."

Carlisle nodded his head slowly. "Yeah, but now I think we might need to take care of that problem."

"We have people to do that. You don't have to get your hands dirty."

"No, I don't, but I don't know if I can go through with it, letting the right people know."

Silent understanding passed between the two of them. There wasn't anything that Carter could say to help Carlisle, and Carlisle wasn't asking for help.

"Let me know if you want me to do anything," Carter offered.

"I do need one thing."

"Oh? What's that?"

"An alibi."

"When the time comes, brother, you'll have one."

"Thanks."

"Yup." Carter picked up his beer bottle and tapped it against Carlisle's. "Brothers, always."

The door to the house opened, and Anabella and Nadia came walking outside. Both of them had smiles on their faces. The men sat up straight in the swings and welcomed their wives over to them.

"Nadia, you are looking rather glowing tonight," Carter said to his sister-in-law.

"Thanks, I feel fantastic."

"There is something about her hair that's different. I've been pestering her all evening about it," Carlisle said.

"Only he would take such notice in my hair." Nadia laughed.

Anabella looked over at her sister and ran her hands through Nadia's hair. "You know, sis, I think your crazy husband is right. Something is up with your hair."

Nadia pawed at her sister to get Anabella's hands out of her hair and stepped backwards one step. "Stop it, you guys. There is nothing wrong with me."

Carlisle stood up, walked towards his wife, and pulled her close to him once he was able to wrap his arm around her waist. "You keep arguing, which makes me think something is up."

Carter pulled out his cell phone and started to google "What causes a woman to glow?" and the first response that came to the top of the google search was "mothers' glow." Carter smiled and looked up at Nadia. He watched her and Carlisle laughing and teasing each other, and he looked to his own wife and grinned. She came over to him and kissed his lips softly.

"Why are you grinning, Carter?"

He simply showed her his cell phone and smiled.

"Ahh!" Anabella screamed at the top of her lungs. Nadia and Carlisle turned to her, and then suddenly, Kain, the boys, and their parents came rushing out of the house.

"What happened? Who's hurt?" Kain said.

"Nadia's pregnant!" Anabella blurted out.

"What?! No I am not!" Nadia protested.

"Yes, you are! Your hair's different. You're glowing. You're acting all lovey-dovey. You're pregnant!"

"By God, say it's so!" William belted out.

"What makes you think that, Ana?" Carlisle asked.

Nadia looked from her sister to her husband, who had the largest grin on his face. "Carlisle!"

"Is it true, my pet?" he asked her in a loving and soothing tone.

"Carlisle..." she whispered.

"It's true, isn't it?"

"I didn't want to tell you, like this. I'm not very far along, just a couple weeks. I tried to tell you in Africa, during the earthquake but you never let me tell you what I needed to tell you."

Carlisle let out a loud holler, leaned down, and swept Nadia off of her feet. "We're having a baby!"

Carter felt his heart warm. He was happy for his new family. He had never thought of things like this before. It had never occurred to him that he would be able to have these simple things in life.

"Aunt Dia!" Daman screamed out. Everyone turned and looked at him in silence. "How're you going to have a baby? Did someone put it in you?"

The backyard became silent. Everyone's gaze went to Kain who burst out into laugher. There wasn't much else someone could say to ease the tension in the moment.

"Daman, I'll tell you when you get older," Kain said.

"He always says that," Daman sighed.

"Come on, kid. I'll tell you how it happens," his older brother, Leon, declared as he took Daman's hand and walked off towards the house.

"I wonder how that conversation is going to go," Laura said, laughing.

"To be a fly on that wall," William agreed.

"Hey, at least he's telling him about the birds and bees and not some kid at school."

Laura looked over at her eldest daughter and grinned. "Now, when are we going to have you two tie the knot officially? We need to plan a huge celebration!"

"We haven't gotten that far in the planning, Mrs. Maverick."

"I hope you two won't be waiting a long time before making it official," William said.

"Dad, why don't you let us settle in for a week, and then we can start the wedding plans."

"I can agree to that," William said, beaming at his daughter.

Carter already loved these people, his new family. He could see that he might have to give up half of his time in Houston, because he couldn't make Anabella move away from all of them.

"Uncle Carlisle did what?!" all of the adults heard Daman shout.

Nadia and Carlisle's faces both flushed red as Daman came running back outside.

Daman's face was serious, and he held his hand up with his finger pointed straight at his aunt and uncle. "Ew, you two need to get a room!"

CHAPTER THIRTEEN

Excitement had taken over the Maverick household over the last twenty-four hours. They had gained a son and had the news of a future grandchild. Laura had cooked a fabulous dinner in celebration of the news of Anabella's upcoming official marriage, and now William and his wife were lying in bed. He hadn't been able today to properly reflect on everything that had transpired. He loved that his girls were happy, but he worried about Kain and the boys. Three men alone in a house needed a woman. That would be what William worked on this next year, since both his daughters were now taken care of.

"You look deep in thought, William," Laura said with a concerned tone.

"I am."

"Care to share?" She curled up alongside him. Her hand came out and rested on top of his heart.

"Thinking about Kain is all."

"What about him?"

"That he and the boys need a woman."

"I think they are doing pretty well on their own, don't you?"

William turned and looked into his wife's eyes. He loved how they sparkled, even in the dim light. There was nothing in the world more important to him that the love of his wife. Not even his children and grandchildren completed him like she did.

"It isn't that they aren't doing well. It's that a man should have a woman to be with, like this. Kain can't get from his sons what I get from you."

"I am not sure he's ready to move on yet."

"He's been divorced for over a year now."

"But no one knows that but you and I. The girls don't know that Deanne isn't coming out of the hospital, and of course Daman and Leon would be heartbroken if they realized it."

William nodded at his wife. "I know all that, but when I have you here in my arms, and I think about my children, I can't help want for them what you and I have."

"Give him time. He will find someone when he is ready and when the boys are ready."

"He's going to have to tell them sooner or later. You know that, right?"

"Of course I do, but how do you tell an eight and eleven year old their mother isn't coming home because she isn't mentally stable?"

"I don't know, Laura. It wasn't her fault she lost control with Kain."

"She tried to kill him. What if the boys had been home?!"

"All the more reason for him to be over her." William rubbed the bridge of his nose and sighed. "I just worry, Laura."

"I know you do, but I think giving him time is important. She's been gone for three years. He will move on when he's ready."

"Goodnight, love." William reached over and turned the lamp off. He pulled her close and held onto the woman he loved. The last thing he thought about was talking to Carlisle. If anyone could help change the course Kain was on, it was him.

Sleep came and went in a blink of an eye for William. It felt like he had just shut his eyes, thinking about his son and son-in-law, when light started to shine through his bedroom. He looked to his right and noticed an emptiness that was present because his wife was missing. He pushed himself up in bed and stretched out his arms wide, inhaling a deep breath. There was a smell of eggs and bacon coming through the room. It reminded him of the old Folgers commercials from the 80's.

When he got out of bed, he saw his slippers and robe were neatly placed in the chair across the room. Laura always took care of him in every way. He was the luckiest man. With a quick look at the clock, he saw it was only 7:14 a.m., and he knew Nadia and Carlisle were awake. Just like her mother, Nadia woke up with the roosters.

William pulled his cell phone off of the charger, punched in Carlisle's name, and hit send. After two rings, he heard his son-in-law answer, saying, "Good Morning."

"Hello, my boy," he said in response to Carlisle's greeting.

"Is everything okay?" Carlisle said with concern.

"A man can't call his son-in-law just to say hello?"

"Not before ten in the morning he can't."

"Aren't you lucky I'm not a normal father-in-law then?"

"I think you mean aren't you lucky I am so laid back for a son-in-law."

"We'll see about that. Now you have competition. Carter may turn out to be the favorite after all."

"Doubtful, but continue, sir. What can I do for you?"

"I want you to check on Kain."

"Check on how? Did something happen to him while we were gone?"

"Not exactly something that happened recently. I'm just worried about him."

"Is this about the divorce? Did you just find out?" Carlisle asked.

"How did you know about that?" William was shocked that Kain had told them. He had said he was keeping it a secret until he could tell the boys.

"They don't call me Mr. A for nothing, William."

"Somehow I always forget what you do for a living."

"It is best you forget that. So, is that what this is regarding?"

William let out a sigh. "Yes and no."

"I'm going to need more information to go off of."

"I want you to check on Kain to see if he is moving on okay. It has been three years since she went away. It's time he moved on. He needs a woman."

"I think Kain is plenty old enough to find his own dates without his brother-in-law playing wingman."

"I'm not talking about you playing wingman. Just simply check on him and make sure he is moving on okay."

"I will see what I can do."

"Thank you. That's all I ask."

Laura's voice traveled up the staircase and into his bedroom, causing him to stop talking. "William, are you talking to someone?"

"I gotta run, Carlisle. Thanks for the help, and please keep this under wraps."

He hung up without waiting for a reply. "You must be hearing the television, Laura. I'm coming down for breakfast."

As he walked into the kitchen, he smiled at Laura and saw his plate ready on the table. "You spoil me, woman."

"I know. Now eat." She walked over and placed a soft kiss on the top of his head. He knew she loved him just as much as he loved her, and that was all the comfort he needed, for now.

"Who was that on the phone?" Nadia asked Carlisle as she walked out of the bathroom and joined him on the couch.

"I don't think I'm supposed to tell you..." he said in a playful tone.

"We don't have any secrets, Mr. Ali," Nadia teased back.

He pulled her closer to him, kissed her nose, and then playfully bit it. "Technically, you already know part of this secret."

She pulled back and raised one eyebrow at him inquisitively.

"Kain and the divorce. That was your father wanting me to check on him. I brought up the divorce, and he reacted as if no one was supposed to know about it, so since you technically know about it..."

"Why does he want you to check up on Kain? Is something wrong?" Her tone turned from playful to worried.

"Who knows? He didn't give any indication that something was wrong. It sounded more like just a worried and concerned father."

"Asking his assassin son-in-law for help." Nadia laughed. "I suppose, if he was going to need a favor, this is a way better favor than it could have been."

"Isn't that the truth?" He picked up the remote and pressed play. He had paused The Twilight Zone when Nadia had stepped into the bathroom, and they had one more episode to finish before he went out for the day to meet Tavin. He hadn't been happy when he'd gotten the text message at six-thirty this morning that they needed to meet, but he couldn't let the boy down. He just wished Tavin could have waited at least until the sun was up in the sky before waking him up.

Nadia and Carlisle spent the next forty minutes in silence as The Twilight Zone played on the television. When it was over, Carlisle realized Nadia had fallen back to sleep in his arms and that was the reason she had been so quiet. He carefully lifted her into his arms and carried her back to their bed. She was going back to the newspaper tomorrow, and he knew she was still exhausted from their travel to Africa.

After making sure she was taken care of, Carlisle slipped out of the house and into his car. Tavin said he was in town and walking around the local Wal-Mart. How weird that must look to the everyday people, a random man just wandering around, but there was no better place to hide than in plain sight.

It took all of ten minutes for him to park and head into the store. He started at the fruit section, looking around for the familiar face. Everyone around him was potentially a future target. That's what made the hobby of people watching so enjoyable, being able to sit and imagine what each person's life was like, before he walked into it.

"Mr. A."

He heard a young voice say his name and turned around with a slow yet powerful movement.

"Mr. T," Carlisle returned, drawing out a long, exaggerated syllable. He grinned and pushed his arm out, exposing his open hand. "Nice to see you again."

"Thank you for meeting me on such short notice."

"That's what we do. Why don't we pay for our few items and go to a less conspicuous place?"

Tavin nodded and waved his arm in the direction of the checkout stands, and Carlisle nodded towards him. He wasn't about to turn his back on anyone, no matter how friendly they were, unless it was Nadia or Carter.

Once their items were paid for, Carlisle gestured towards his vehicle in the parking lot, and Tavin followed.

"You still don't trust me?" Tavin asked.

"It isn't about trust in this business. It's about life and if I am willing to put mine in your hands."

"I've been trained. I'm part of the brotherhood."

Carlisle looked over at him as he started up his engine. "That doesn't make you my brother." As he pulled out of his parking spot and began to drive out of the parking lot and onto the road, he said in a cool tone, "Being a brother is about shared experiences. We have none."

"That's partially the reason I am here."

He took a sidelong glance at Tavin before deciding to say nothing. He drove them back to his home. He didn't know of a more secure location, even though he didn't want to expose Nadia to any danger. He pulled his car into the back side of the house and opened the garage with one press of a button.

"My wife is asleep. Please remain silent until we are in my work room."

Tavin nodded his head, and they both exited the car. The doors shut with virtual silence, and they made their way through the downstairs and into the basement without awakening Nadia. Carlisle pulled around a spare chair for Tavin to sit down. When he moved to his desk, he pressed a button along his bookshelf, and the door closed behind them.

"This is quite the set up you have, Mr. A."

"Thank you. It's taken me a few years to make this house just how I needed it. I'm quite proud."

"I hope to be like you one day."

Carlisle let his thumb and forefinger run along both sides of his jawline. He thought about what this young man had said to him before responding. "How long have you been in our industry?"

"Couple years."

"You're acting very friendly with me, as if it had been longer."

"Don't mean to insult you."

"No," Carlisle said, "I don't think you do. I think you need something."

"I..." Tavin paused.

"Need a favor, yes?" Carlisle finished his sentence.

Tavin slowly nodded his head twice. "I do." He let out a long sigh.

"Tell me what's going on, brother."

Tavin's hand came up to the top of his head and he tousled his own hair. "It's not for me. It's for Sasha."

"What's wrong with your sister?" This is why they didn't take people into the brotherhood when they had a family, Carlisle thought to himself, too much risk, weakness. "Is she hurt?"

"She isn't hurt."

"Has she been kidnapped?"

"She hasn't been kidnapped."

"Then what do you need help with? Is she locked up?"

Tavin lowered his head at that one. That was it. She was locked up.

"How do you want my assistance, Tavin?"

"She's innocent. I need help proving she didn't do the crime she is in jail for right now."

"And what crime is she in jail for?"

"Theft. She bought a necklace from someone, and it ended up being stolen property. She was caught in possession of it, and now they are going to convict her if I can't get her charges dropped."

"How do you know she is innocent?"

"Sasha is my sister. Don't you think I would know if she was capable of stealing something?"

"You and I don't look like we are capable of killing people, and that's our job. That's why I question you. Okay, so tell me what you want me to do? Are we breaking her out of jail, or are we proving her innocent?"

"I want to prove her innocent, but worst case, I want to break her out and put her into hiding somewhere safe."

"I'm going to have to think this through. This is going to affect more than just you. It is pushing me into an area I haven't really been in before."

"But you'll do it?"

"Yeah, I will," Carlisle said hesitantly. How would this new job change his views on things in the legal system? He didn't usually care about the innocent, just the guilty going free.

"I'll pay whatever is needed to do this too, no expense spared."

Carlisle looked over at Tavin. He had almost forgotten he was in the room with him until he started to speak again. "I won't charge for this service."

"You don't even know how long this is going to take you to do, or what expenses you are going to encounter. I have to pay you."

"Brother's do favors for brothers, and you are claiming we are brothers, right?"

Tavin nodded his head yes.

"Then it's settled. I'll be in touch once I have a plan." Carlisle pushed away from his desk and stood up. He began walking to the door.

"Don't you want to know about the case?"

"No."

"How will you know what you need to know?"

Carlisle opened the door and smiled. "I have my ways. Let me take you back to your car."

"If you say so..." Tavin walked out of the house and got into the car.

The two men drove back to the Wal-Mart in silence, neither of them saying anything. Carlisle dropped Tavin off at his car in the parking lot. He was about to drive away when Tavin stuck his head back inside of the car. "Thank you, Carlisle."

"It's Mr. A, and no problem." He paused for a moment and then said, "When I get Sasha out on bail, make sure you bring her to the party when you get the upcoming invite from me. It will be good for me to meet her unofficially as your friend before she finds out I'm investigating. She'll be easier to get a read on."

"Yes, sir."

Carlisle arrived back home and this time found Nadia standing in the kitchen looking at the refrigerator with a very intense stare.

"Something wrong, my pet?" he asked

"Yeah, I think there is something spoiled in here, but I can't find the source, and the smell isn't quite awful yet, so I can't totally track it down."

Carlisle smiled widely; he loved when it was the simple things in life that drove her nuts. Those were easy to fix. "We can just throw it all out and start fresh. Don't stress." He walked over to her and wrapped his arms around her, letting her back press up against his chest.

"We are not throwing out all of this food! I won't be wasteful, but that smell, I just can't get it out of my head."

"I'm sure you will find it. Let's go chill in the living room; we can watch some more TWZ."

"TWZ? What?" Nadia looked over her shoulders at him with a questioning glare.

"Twilight Zone. Get it? TWZ? Thought I would shorten things."

"I think you were mistaken. We don't shorten The Twilight Zone." Nadia turned around in his arms and laughed. She wrapped her arms around his neck, leaned into him, and placed a kiss on his lips.

"What was that for, Mrs. Ali?"

"Because I missed you. Where did you go?"

"Who said I went anywhere?" He kissed her back, hoping to distract her.

"The little alarm that beeps when doors open and close around here. That's who said you left."

"Blast those little buggers!"

Nadia's laughter filled the kitchen, and that filled his heart. Seeing and hearing her happiness made life worthwhile.

"I actually wanted to talk to you about it. Why don't we go into the living room and cuddle while I tell you about a young protégé named Tavin Thomas and his sister Sasha."

CHAPTER FOURTEEN

Nadia listened to Carlisle explain the conversation he had just had with Tavin. She didn't know what to think of this new person that was suddenly putting himself into their lives. If she was honest with herself, she knew that there were others out there that did the same job Carlisle did, but she didn't want to ever admit what it was they did, and now more of them were inserting themselves into her world. Carter seemed different. Maybe it was because he was older and looked like he was well put together.

She wasn't sure, but this new person wasn't going to be the same as Carter. Nadia knew that the instant she heard his age. She didn't want anything to do with him, but she wasn't sure how to tell Carlisle.

"Nadia, is something wrong?" Carlisle stopped talking and waited patiently for her to respond.

With a slow shake of her head she said, "No, not really. Why?"

"You've been staring off into space this entire time. Did you hear what I said?"

"I did. I just don't know what to think about this new development."

She watched Carlisle nod his head in agreement, and that made her feel a little better about everything.

Nadia paid close attention to him and then asked, "What don't you like about it?"

"All of it. We just got home from a vacation that should have been exciting and relaxing but instead was stressful and almost killed. I really just wanted to relax for a while."

"Then why did you leave yesterday?" she asked.

"When I went to get new stuff?"

Nadia nodded.

"I didn't think you knew..."

She cut him off. "I always know. I just sometimes act like I don't."

Carlisle let out an audible sigh. "Why didn't you say anything?"

"You didn't want to tell me. I wasn't going to tell you I knew. I always know when you're off doing what it is you do."

"Well, since you know that..." He paused a moment and ran his hand through his hair. "Tavin is the one who asked me to go out and do a job."

"Do you want to tell me more details about the job, maybe more specifics?"

He gave her a look that pretty much said Yes, I do, but I can't. Nadia just nodded in understanding. "What can you tell me?"

"I didn't do it."

"Do what?" Nadia's voice had a bit of worry in it, and he didn't know what to make of that exactly. What was she worried about? Was she worried for him? For what he didn't do? Or was she worried that finally his profession was beginning to weigh on her?

"I didn't do the assignment. I didn't feel comfortable with it, so I punted it back to Tavin and came home. Well, I did some shopping first, but I turned it down."

"Is that going to hurt you in the future?"

Carlisle shook his head. "Why would it hurt me?"

She shrugged. "I don't exactly know how this whole thing works. How it all works. Hell, I don't even know how you get paid!"

This made Carlisle laugh out loud. She loved hearing him laugh, but right now wasn't exactly the right time for it. "Do you want to know how I get paid, Nadia?"

"Yes." She paused. "No," she said. "Maybe," she settled on.

"How about I just simply tell you there are powers out there in the world who pay me monthly to keep my end of the deal up."

"What happens when like yesterday you refuse?"

"Nothing, they will look at the reasons I gave and investigate the initial claim."

"And what if you reject the next assignment and the next one?"

Carlisle smiled at her and began to explain how the process worked. "After three rejections in a two month span, you are summoned to a meeting where you sit down and discuss what is going on. Sometimes that starts the process of retirement, other times it just clears the air and gives someone a new source."

Nadia gulped. "Retirement?" She felt her heart start to speed up. "They don't..." She couldn't finish the sentence, and when Carlisle started laughing again, she got angry. "Why are you laughing?!"

"Nadia, honey, they don't kill you! They just retire you, like if you were an accountant." He didn't think she needed to know what happened to the leaders when they became careless in 'retirement'.

She let him pull her close and felt some comfort as he wrapped his arms around her and began to rock slowly with her. "I promise you, Nadia, no one will ever take me away from you, ever."

"I know." She nuzzled her head into Carlisle's chest, simply enjoying his warmth. "I guess this kind of touched a nerve. I worry about losing you."

She felt him kiss the top of her head. "My pet, you won't ever lose me."

"I love you."

"I love you too, Nadia."

The night was emotional for Carlisle and Nadia. After their heart to heart, they spent the rest of the night in bed, cuddling. Nadia kept crying off and on, thinking about their talk. Carlisle didn't know how to stop it. Nadia insisted all night it was the hormones and that there wasn't anything he could do to make the crying valve shut off, but he didn't like it any more knowing it wasn't under her control.

An idea had occurred to him while he was lying in bed, though, how he could help Tavin and possibly his dear father-in-law. He could give Kain a project, an investigative one. He could help Carlisle with this project, and that would give Carlisle a reason to spend some time with him, to check on him.

He felt good about this plan and decided that, once Nadia left for work, he would go about contacting Kain and setting up the first step in operation distraction. He heard her coming into the room he was in, and she looked smashing.

"You're going to report on the news in that?" he asked. She wore a long red dress, one that fit snug around her hips. It helped to accentuate the features he had come to love about her. The top was sleeveless and the scoop neck showed off a little more of her chest than he would have normally liked.

"Do I not look okay?" she questioned back.

"It isn't that. It's just, the men are going to stare..." He walked up to her, pulled her close, and kissed her.

"That's exactly the response I am hoping for."

"I don't understand. You are writing a news article. What do you need to dress up for?"

"I thought you'd never ask!" Nadia jumped back with excitement in her eyes and her voice. "I've been asked to guest host a talk show!"

"A talk show?"

She nodded firmly. "A talk show!"

"What show?" He didn't know how he felt about this. She was already an easy target, and now the world would see her on television. He would have to keep watch on her twenty-four seven.

"It's our local station's lunch talk show. Isn't it exciting?! I got a call this morning when I didn't reply to an email I got yesterday. It had gone to my junk folder, so I didn't even see it!" She twirled around, "How do I look, honestly? Is this too much?"

"I'd say it is definitely not enough. You could use a few more inches of material on your body."

Nadia let out a loud laugh and twirled around again. "This is so exciting. A talk show host, me!"

"Guest talk show host, my pet. What will your topics be?"

She shrugged. "Who knows? Who cares? It's gonna be great! I gotta go call Mom and Ana. They are gonna get a kick outta it!"

Carlisle laughed, moved closer to her, and kissed her again, this time with a bit more passion. "So I've married a star, huh?"

"I've always been a star. Now everyone is just going to see me."

"Lord help us," he said under his breath.

Nadia smiled and waved goodbye as she walked out of the room. He heard her shut the garage door and the outer door open. He moved to the window and watched her drive off. She did have a special way of lightening up a room with her energy.

Once she was free and clear of the driveway, Carlisle took this opportunity to get ahold of Kain. He pulled out his cell phone and scrolled through a few names until his brother-in-law's appeared on the screen. As he waited for the phones to connect and ring, he thought about how he was going to broach this topic with him.

Three rings later, he heard the familiar voice on the other end. "Hey, Carlisle."

"Hello, Kain. How are you doing?"

"I'm fine, just staying busy. How about you? You guys all settled in from the big adventure in Africa?"

"Let's not talk about what a disaster that trip turned out to be."

"It couldn't have been a total disaster!"

"Trust me, the only thing positive out of this trip was finding out I'm going to be a dad."

"Well see? Told you it wasn't all a disaster."

"Good point, old man." Carlisle laughed.

"Hey, watch it. Aren't we the same age?"

"I'll never tell you."

It was now Kain's turn to laugh. "I'll just get it out of Nadia."

"You're lucky you know my birthday at all."

"December 5th, two days before Pearl Harbor."

"Yeah, 'cause that's what I want people thinking about when they think of me, total destruction."

"Well..." Kain paused and laughed harder.

"Touché, brother."

"So what did you need, Carlisle? You don't normally call to shoot the shit. Nadia okay?"

"Yeah, she's fine. Did you hear yet? She's going to be on the local talk show today as a co-host. She left out of the house all smiling and wearing a dress she really needed to keep for a more private occasion. Far too much skin showing."

"Yeah, those Maverick women tend to overdo it a bit, but no, she hadn't called and told me. What a brat!"

"I'm sure you're next on her list to call."

"Then why are you calling?"

Carlisle let a moment or two of silence lapse before speaking again. "I need a favor."

"From me?" Kain almost sounded shocked.

"Yeah."

"Now I'm intrigued. What can I do for you?"

"I have a..." he paused as he considered what he should call Tavin, "an associate who is in need of some investigative help, and he's asked me for it."

"Okay, where do I fit in?"

"I wanted to see if I could get you to help me do a bit of reconnaissance on this job."

"I think you meant to call Gabe and Kevin. What can I do for you?"

"It isn't hard work, just some research and a bit of snooping and what not. You've done odd jobs here and there. I thought, why not?"

"Did Dad call you?"

"William? Why would he call me?" Carlisle tried to play his tone off as if he was shocked by the accusation.

"Uh huh..." Kain paused. "Dad is calling everyone. He wants me to stay busy. I'm not sure what has flown up in his head that makes him think I need to be taken care of. I'm perfectly fine."

"I'm sure your dad just worries."

"Again, uh huh. What did he ask you to do?"

Carlisle sighed. "He asked me to keep you busy with something."

"And does this friend of yours really need help?"

"Actually, yes, he does. Well, his sister does."

Kain paused for a few seconds. Carlisle wasn't sure what his brother-in-law was going to say.

"Fine, give me the details. I'll help you out, but only because I am curious as to what your friends are like."

"He isn't a friend so much as an associate."

"Even better," Kain replied.

Carlisle went on to give Kain the bit of information that he had. He wasn't sure if it would be enough to go on, but he thought, why not let him try.

They hung up the phone in good spirits and agreed to talk some more that night at the big party. Carlisle now felt obligated to call

William and let him know that he had now done his part in William's scheme.

When he lifted his phone once more, he began to pull the name up but didn't want to get stuck having to explain what kind of task he had found for Kain to do, so he simply opened up a text message and shot William a quick line.

Kain's being detained. Mission accomplished.

Hopefully that was going to be enough to appease the eldest Maverick. If it wasn't, then Carlisle would just have to find something else to tell him.

Nadia's left leg couldn't stop bouncing up and down as she sat in the studio waiting for the makeup personnel to leave her alone. The more she stared up at the clock, the more anxious she got. She could almost hear the second hand ticking by second by second as it got closer to show time. The studio had set her up in the guest room. The front door had masking tape outside of it with "Mrs. Nadia Ali" written on the front. She was looking at the back of the door when she heard a knock.

"Come in," she called out.

When the door opened, she saw her mother and sister peeking their heads around the wooden door, smiling at her. "Where's our TV star?" her mother called out.

"I'm not a star, just a guest!" she replied, giggling and smiling at her family.

"My sister, the star! Pretty soon you will have your own star on the walk of fame."

"Now who's getting away with themselves?!" Nadia shooed away the makeup people and turned her chair around to see her mother and sister. "How do I look?"

Her mother gave her the once over and shook her head. "We can't tell anything with you sitting down. Stand up and give us a twirl." Laura twisted her finger in a circle as she spoke.

Nadia hopped out of the chair, raised her body up on her tip toes, and spun. The dress clung to her legs and shone in the light as the women in the room squealed with delight.

"Darling, you look perfect." Laura hugged her daughter tightly.

"Mom, can't you see the glow?" Anabella said as she peered at her sister.

Laura nodded and all three women looked into the mirror. "You're a beautiful pregnant bride, Nadia."

"Mom, I'm not a bride. We've been married over a year!"

"You're still his bride," she said calmly.

"That's right. You're still my bride."

All three women's heads spun around towards the back as Carlisle pushed open the door as he was speaking.

"You came..." Nadia said.

"Of course I came. Do you think I could pass this up?"

As he pushed open the door, Nadia's father and Carter both stepped into the picture. Her eyes began to tear up, and she started to fan herself. "No, no, not the makeup!"

Then, as if on cue, Daman and Leon came running into the room, each carrying a bouquet of roses.

"Aunt Dia, Aunt Dia! I picked these outs just for you!" Daman hollered.

She leaned over and scooped both boys into a big hug and then gathered up the roses and smelled them. "This is going to make me cry more." She looked up and saw her big brother walking into the room, stepping over the threshold with a beaming smile. Carter came into focus, following shortly behind him.

"Hey, kid, lookin' good," he told her.

"I love you guys. You all didn't have to come."

"We've been standing in that hallway forever, Aunt Nadia. Uncle A said we all had to surprise you and couldn't come in all at once."

Nadia looked over at her husband and then to the rest of the family. She finally let the tears form and roll down her cheeks.

"Mrs. Ali, here's your five minute warning," a small man with a microphone and earpiece set on his head said as he walked into the now full dressing room. "Oh my, what happened? Your mascara has run!" he declared.

Laura and Anabella both turned their heads quickly and looked over Nadia's face. Her mother waved him off and told him she'd be ready in three minutes. The women pushed all the men back and went to work, doctoring up her makeup.

Someone should have timed them, because Nadia swore that it was faster than three minutes. It felt like ninety seconds at most. She looked herself over in the mirror a couple times before considering her face back to normal. When she turned around, she noticed that Carlisle was waiting at the door with his arm extended to escort her down to the taping area. She said goodbye to her family and went to her husband. She slipped her arm into his, and they began walking.

They made it down the corridor in silence, and as she was about to push open the studio door, he placed his open palm on the side of her face, leaned down, and kissed her. "Break a leg, my pet. I love you."

"I love you too, Mr. A."

She could hear the studio audience from outside in the hallway, so she knew it was already buzzing, alive with energy. She pushed open the studio door and began walking out onto the stage where she was greeted with a warm smile and a friendly hug.

"Are you ready for all this, Nadia?"

She nodded her head a few times and smiled. "Sure am, Carly. Just tell me which direction to look in."

CHAPTER FIFTEEN

"You have to be careful where you step when you are hunting for the story, Carly. You never know what pile you're going to run your feet through!" Nadia said as the audience started into a calm, yet appropriate laugh.

"Oh Nadia, you're quite descriptive with your word choices," Carly said in a quick retort.

"Gotta be in my kind of work, Carly."

"I am sure you do." Carly looked deep into the camera in front of the two women and smiled. "Cedar Rapids, this has been Carly Silva and Nadia Ali giving you your lunchtime break. We hope that the entertainment keeps you on your toes and out of trouble. Enjoy the rest of your day!"

When the lights dimmed and the cameras turned off, Nadia stood up, smiling ear to ear. She saw her family sitting in the front row and rushed over to them.

"That was great, Nadia!" Anabella said first.

"You looked stunning!" Laura proclaimed.

"Aunt Dia! We loved you!" Daman squealed.

"Thank you, guys! It was so much fun, but God! I was so nervous."

"Breathtakingly perfect as always, love." She heard the sound of her best friend's voice and smiled up at him. He was always there for her, even when she didn't know it.

"You made it!" Nadia proclaimed. Her smile grew even wider than it had just been.

"Nadia?" Carly called from the set.

Everyone's attention focused on the show's beautiful host. Nadia stepped forward, away from the Maverick clan, and smiled. "Thank you so much, Carly."

"No, it's I who should thank you. That was more fun than I've had in a long time!" When Carly was standing right in front of Nadia, she wrapped her arms around her, giving her a quick hug. "Thanks so much for this! I think you may need to become a regular."

"A regular?!" Nadia exclaimed. "I hope you're joking."

"Hardly. I'll talk to my station manager, but once the ratings come out, I am sure we will be booking you as a co-host from now on. Trust me, I know these things. There are the women who simply report the news, and then there are women like you, who make the news."

"Aunt Dia, you've becomes a star!"

Everyone turned their heads towards Kain's youngest son and laughed in unison.

"Daman, you twit, she isn't a star yet. She was just offered a job," Leon corrected.

"Leon!" Laura, Anabella, Nadia, and Kain all yelled at once.

He turned around and shrugged his shoulders. "What? It's the truth."

"Come on, son. Let's go talk about that language you seem to love throwing about." Kain nodded his head in Nadia's direction, and her heart pained a little for her nephew. She knew he was going through a rough spot with his parents' divorce being final, and she wished she could help shield him.

"Well, what do you say, Nadia?" Carly brought the attention back to the main point.

"I, uh, I..." She looked over at her husband, who had remained mostly silent throughout most of this. "Carlisle?"

"My pet, you can do whatever you want."

She smiled at him and then turned to Carly. "You need to know I'm pregnant. I'm going to get all fat and moody."

Anabella coughed and smiled. "She's already moody."

Carter wrapped his arm around her and shushed her as he pulled her close to him.

Nadia let out another nervous laugh and nodded her head. "Okay, yes, yes, I'll do it!"

"Wonderful!" Carly gave her another hug and then stepped away. "I'll have my station manager call you with the details tomorrow. Enjoy the rest of the day with your family."

As Carly walked away, Nadia felt her stomach start to turn circles. She wasn't sure if this was a result of the pregnancy or just being placed in the center spotlight for an hour, but she needed to take a break.

"Are we ready to go now?" she asked Carlisle.

"Yes, but I promised your mother we would have lunch with her." Carlisle looked over at her mom and dad, and suddenly, something felt off.

"Okay..." she said nervously.

"Ana, do you want to join them for lunch?" Carter said. Nadia could tell this was a fake impromptu comment.

"Sure! Mom, is that okay?"

Laura nodded and looked at the whole Maverick group. "Yes, why don't you all come over?"

"Great idea, Laura!" William replied to his wife.

"We'll meet you there." Carlisle put his hand under Nadia's elbow and began to move her away from their family.

As they walked towards her dressing room, she stopped in the hallway and gave him a stern look. "What's going on?"

"Nothing, my pet. Come on. Let's get your things."

He tried to force her to move by placing her elbow back in his palm, but she moved her arm in a circular motion and forced him to release her. "I know when you're hiding something," she said.

"I'm not hiding anything, Nadia."

She looked at him carefully, as if examining him. "Fine, but I'm making a note that I am calling you out on some B.S. right now."

"Noted. Now come on, before we get locked in this place."

"Locked in? It's in the middle of the day."

"Never know," he simply stated.

She decided that protesting wasn't going to get her anywhere, so she let it go. They went into her dressing room, grabbed her bag, and then headed towards her car.

The memories of everything that just happened were playing in her head. She couldn't believe that in a short morning so much of her life was about to change. She loved being a reporter, but she and Carlisle had been talking about it before they left for Africa. The scene could be a dangerous one, and he was ready for her to reconsider her life's passion.

Technically, she agreed with him. At first, Nadia had felt it was a bit hypocritical, given everything, but since she had found out she was pregnant, that had all been changing in her mind.

Then her mind went to Gabe, her best friend. She had worked with him for as long as she could remember and didn't know what she would do without him. That saddened her. He would probably take it the hardest, her changing professions.

She was sure Scully would be relieved about never having to run interference between her and the police again.

"You look very deep in thought."

"I am." She had a very low tone about her. Her heart started to feel heavy, and tears started to form in her eyes. She was already sick of crying, and she had eight more months of this left.

"What are you thinking about?"

"Nothing, I promise."

"Okay. Well, you will enjoy lunch with your family."

"I always enjoy time with my family."

They drove the remainder of the short distance in silence. As they pulled into her parents' driveway, she noticed that everyone was already there. "Wow, did everyone speed here or something?"

"Maybe I just drove slowly?" Carlisle offered.

She shook it off and started to walk up the driveway of her parents' house and along the path to their front door. Carlisle had moved quickly from the car and now was standing behind her. She saw him press the doorbell and thought that was out of character. "Why ring? We always walk right on in," she said as she opened the door.

When she looked into the living room she saw all of the decorations and her family looking back, smiling at her. The wall said "Congratulations!" in blue and pink balloons. There were blue and pink storks taped up on the walls, and her nephews held presents in their hands.

The tears came full on now. She didn't hold them back. She felt Carlisle's arm wrap around her tightly and that brought her comfort. She knew how much she was loved. Her hands drifted down to her stomach, which hadn't begun to show on the outside but inside held her special little light.

Laura and William walked over to her, and they wrapped their arms around both Nadia and Carlisle. The warm embrace was perfect, and she knew this future grandchild would already be the most loved baby in the world.

"We decided on a party for you, Aunt Dia!"

"It was Dad's idea, but Daman and I helped decorate," Leon said, smiling.

"Open our presents, Aunt Dia!" Leon moved out of the way as Daman came running at her and Carlisle.

Carlisle knelt down on the floor, and Nadia watched him smile at their nephew. "Thank you," he told Daman.

"Hopes you like it, Uncle Carlisle." Daman was beaming a bright smile that radiated throughout the room.

He slowly slipped his finger under the wrapping paper. "Did you wrap it yourself?" he asked Daman.

The little brown haired boy nodded up and down vigorously. "You did a great job, little man."

Carlisle finished unwrapping the present. It was a cream colored box. Inside of it was a silver picture frame. Inside there was a photo of Nadia and Daman when he was first born, and next to it there was a spot for another photo. Daman moved to look at the photo. He pointed and said, "This is where you will put a picture of you and your baby, right next to you and me. That way we can be cousins for life."

He looked so proud of himself. Nadia knelt down as well and pulled him in for a long hug.

"That's the most perfect present in the world, little man. I love you so much."

"I love you too, Aunt Dia." Then he sat on the ground and leaned his head close to Nadia's stomach and whispered. "I love you too little cousin. See you soon!"

EPILOGUE

Kain tucked the boys in after a long day at his parents' and the party for Nadia. He loved seeing her happy. She was glowing tonight in a way he had never seen any other woman glow, pregnant or not. He knew that it was a combination of Carlisle's love and the pregnancy, and he was happy for his baby sister.

What he hadn't told anyone in the family yet was that he had gotten a call from his ex-wife's attorney the day before. She was starting to understand what she had done and wanted to see him and apologize. He had told Mr. Schitz that he didn't want to see Deanne again, but he knew that he would have to face her at some point. He did have two sons with her, and at some point, he would have to tell them about what had happened.

Maybe his father had been right; he needed a distraction. He had started to think about what Carlisle had asked of him. He had done a cursory search of Sasha Thomas. What he had found seemed a bit interesting.

Since she was now on his mind, he went into his home office and turned on his desktop. He had never wanted to get a laptop. He felt people who used them tended to take their work with them places that needed to be for relaxation only. He pulled up Google and typed her name into the search engine. After scrolling through the first page of hits, he clicked on the one that brought up the news article on her case. Why people got themselves into these kinds of predicaments was beyond him.

But he was doing this favor for a friend, no, a brother, and that meant he would give this project his all.

"Sasha Thomas, it's time to learn your deep dark secrets…"

Don't miss out!

Click the button below and you can sign up to receive emails whenever Ashley Nemer publishes a new book. There's no charge and no obligation.

https://books2read.com/r/B-A-NDUF-JFMS

BOOKS 2 READ

Connecting independent readers to independent writers.

Also by Ashley Nemer

Kemah Sunrise
HoneySuckle Love

Maverick Touch
Maverick Touch The Cat
Maverick Touch The Highway
Maverick Touch The Adventure
Maverick Touch Jail Break

Novella & Short Stories
Bud's Christmas Wish / Miracle
Under The Moonlight
Wolf Pack

The Blood Series
Blood Purple
Blood Yellow
Blood Green

Blood White

Watch for more at https://www.ashleynemer.com.

About the Author

Ashley is married and lives in Houston with her husband and their two children. She and her husband have been together for over a decade and he brings her more joy than she could ever imagine as a child. Their two children have filled their lives with laughter and excitement on a daily basis. She loves to read and has been hooked on the romance genre ever since her life long best friend Laura gave her "Ashes to Ashes' by Tami Hoag to read when they were in high school.

Ashley finds her strength through her family, especially her parents. They always support her in life, they push her to strive for greatness. There once was a motto that Ashley heard in her youth through her Taekwondo life 'Reach for the Stars' and that is what Ashley has always done. It was through her upbringing that the values Ashley has and display's came from. With her Parents always cheering her on in life she was able to grow up having faith in herself and her ability to conquer the world.

Author Links

http://www.ashleynemer.com

http://www.facebook.com/ashleynemerauthor

http://www.facebook.com/ashers83 (Add Friend)

http://ashleynemer.blogspot.com

https://twitter.com/ashleynemer

https://www.goodreads.com/user/show/2897381-ashley-nemer

Read more at https://www.ashleynemer.com.

ART OF SAFKHET

About the Publisher

SAFKHET READERS

Safkhet's Pride - Our Street Team (Open to twenty (20) members)

Here, readers will interact with the authors and have behind the scene chats to get the word out there about our book releases. We will have contests and special swag that is offered ONLY to our Street Team.

Requirements:

At least once a month post about one of the books released from The Art of Safkhet.

At least once a month share one status by an author.

When a new release comes out, recommend it to at least five friends on Goodreads.

What's in it for you:

All new releases the month they come out will be sold at a discount price. E-books will be 50% off and print books will be 30% off.

When SWAG arrives all members will get first grabs at the items

Special contests for print books or gift cards held just for members of the Street Team.

Safkhet's Elite - Our Beta Readers (Open to fifty (50) readers only)

Here, readers will get advanced readers copy (in e-book format)

Readers will tell us which genre's they want to read and we will email them their ARC.

Genres are:

Paranormal

Contemporary Romance

Erotica

Science Fiction

Mystery

Mythology

Poetry

Requirements:

Upon receiving an advanced copy of our new release, you will need to post your honest review with in fifteen days of its release and place a link to that review on the appropriate authors Facebook page.

If you cannot read the ARC in a timely fashion please email Grace (info@artofsafkhet.com) so she can make note. Missing more than two e-book distributions in a row without reason will have you removed from Safkhet's Elite.

Your review must be honest. We are not looking for all 5-Star reviews but honest opinions and thoughts about our work.

By joining this program you agree to not share, distribute or sell the Advanced Readers Copy of our work.

Some of you will want to be both, a Pride member and an Elite member. At this time we are asking that you pick one or the other. This may change in the future but for right now we ask that you just pick one. If you are interested in either of these please let us know.

You can join Safkhet's Pride by going to this link https://www.facebook.com/groups/222253454608269/. This will take you to our Facebook group where we will post the different information.

You can apply for Safkhet's Elite by commenting on this post with your name, email address and genre's you want to read and stating which of Ashley, Stacy, Anabella, or Niki books you liked most or by sending Grace an email at info@artofsafkhet.com with all of the information.

Thank you for taking the time out to inquire about our new Readers Groups and we hope to see 70 new people in the near future!

Made in the USA
Columbia, SC
27 April 2018